The Felonies

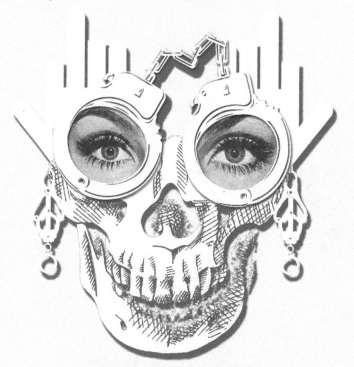

GRINDHOUSE
PRESS

A.S. COOMER

Published by Grindhouse Press
PO BOX 293161
Dayton, Ohio 45429

The Fetishists
Grindhouse Press # 031
ISBN-10: 1-941918-19-0
ISBN-13: 978-1-941918-19-7

For Rachel

NOW

The sun was either exceedingly bright as it crested the dew-topped, pine-knotted ridgeline or, much more likely, the hangover was settling in to be a really nasty one. Jefferson had to look away from it, the sun. It felt like a spotlight directed at his soul, highlighting the previous evening as something like the beginning of the end. The precursor to a life bereft of all potential, hope and promise.

"Shit," Jefferson said, the word vaporizing in the chill, condensing into the ghost of the sibilance which churned up and away from his chattering mouth.

His body shook and another two set of possibilities came to him. One: the cold. Two: he was coming down.

When he'd finished throwing up for the second time, the steam rising back into his face heavy with the smell of bile and bourbon, he wondered for the first time why he was outside. He hadn't ended the night outside as far as his memory—slaggingly halted and hazy though it were that morning—would allow. He'd been inside. At the party.

Oh, God, the party.

THE PREVIOUS EVENING

"The auction block opens."

The words wisped from the speakers tactfully hidden behind panels in the ceiling. A light jazz trickled behind them.

Jefferson took a hefty sip from the glass, a very expensive bourbon, bottled some eighteen years ago, that he'd never even heard of and made his way to the plush seat whose name card indicated it was reserved for him.

He didn't really know anybody at this one, this party. That didn't really bother him. He'd gotten over that years ago. It came with the territory.

Others shuffled to their seats amidst the clinking of ice cubes in glasses and small polite sounding cocktail chitter. Black dresses, some much shorter than others, some leather even, were in great abundance at this one, this party.

Jefferson smiled to himself and vaguely toyed with believing it was from the bourbon, the eighteen-year, though a native Kentuckian, he'd never heard of.

The lights dimmed and a hush settled over the buyers. A small stream of light fell onto a standing podium, behind which stood a tall, rail-thin woman somewhere in her mid-forties, probably. The light blinked off her thick-framed glass-

6

es every time her head dipped toward the spec sheets resting on top of the podium.

Something about the woman struck Jefferson as odd. She was wearing all black, as per the usual protocol, nothing as out-and-out as leather but black and harsh nonetheless. The glasses were clipped onto a thin golden chain that hung around her neck giving her a professorial air. He scanned the lining of the shirt, the black buttons on black wool, and saw it, the oddness. The difference. She had no breasts.

"Cherry, here, would be a great sow for any barnyard. 35C-27-38," the woman at the podium said, her voice low and muted, something from AM radio's past, a sultry, slow-burning talkshow hostess' voice. "Go ahead and moo for us, Cherry."

A high-pitched, wholehearted "moo" came from the darkness beside the podium before a harsh, fluorescent light shone into existence and illuminated the cow, Cherry.

"Moo. Moo."

She was down on all fours on a slowly spinning pedestal. She tossed her head side to side as if warding off flies from the summer pasture.

"Moo," Cherry, the cow, said.

Jefferson sipped from the eighteen year, the bourbon, and smiled to himself.

This is going to be a night to remember, he thought.

NOW

He propped himself against an oak for support. His ears were ringing, his pulse thudding like a club's bass system in his head.

Thump-thump, thump-thump.

"Jesus," he whispered to himself.

He was covered in sweat despite the cold. It stung being simultaneously hot and cold like that. He did his best to look around, slowly, careful not to upset the precarious balance required for a truly royal hangover like this. He didn't know where he was. He didn't see the house.

"Jesus," he whispered again. "How did I get out here?"

He pushed himself off the trunk of the tree and took an unsteady step toward the gentle rise ahead. The sun was, mercifully, shaded by several strands of thick foliage overhead. Two more steps and he had to drop to his knees and empty what was left in his stomach.

When his breathing regained some semblance of regularity, Jefferson sat on his ass, his hands far behind him, his head lolling limply back. He sat like that for some time. Not thinking about how he'd gotten lost in the woods in a part of the county he'd never been in before. Not thinking about how he'd gotten so terribly hungover without any memory of being really drunk in the first place.

He just sat there and thought about not throwing up. That's all. Simply not retching again. His stomach was roiling and he wasn't sure he hadn't already peppered his Jockies with friendly fire.

As he sat forward, curling his legs together, indian-style, the sun found a way through the leaves, splashing onto his face the cruel light of a clear fall morning. He made to cover his eyes with his right hand but saw something strange through his narrowed vision.

"What the—"

He held the hand before his face and saw two missing fingers. Bloody nubs, blackened by some intense heat, some burning, sat where his ring and pinky fingers should have stood.

THE PREVIOUS EVENING

They came on you like shadows in the dark. You could hardly tell they were there. Just when the ice cubes in your glass were all but melted, the eighteen-year, the bourbon, all but gone, they were there.

"Another, sir?"

A disjointed shadow voice in the dark.

The cup was silently, carefully taken and another, chill to the touch, the cubes somehow not even clinking with the motion, inserted into the briefly empty hand.

"Thank you," Jefferson said.

He thought a nod might have been issued from the darkness, the shadows.

"Sold," the woman at the podium said, followed by the firm rap of gavel on wood.

The spinning pedestal stopped. The cow, Cherry, was leashed by her new owner and led, still on all fours, away from the light into the shadows.

"Next, we have another fine barnyard animal, another excellent harem addition or, perhaps, just another painslut for your enjoyment."

A hairy man was led to the pedestal by a leash. He was

shirtless except for twin leather straps, lined with metal studs, leading to a thick diaper looking leather bottom. There was a quivering about the man's movement. He held back just before getting to the pedestal but was forced onto it with one hard jerk by one of the shadow people.

Once the man was fully on it, the pedestal began its slow rotation.

"Four and a half inches, 268 pounds, 5'7". We'll start the bidding at—"

NOW

Jefferson stared at his ruined hand. His mind was amazingly blank for some time. The impossibility of it disallowed any thought. He felt those fingers, the missing ones, the ones no longer attached to his hand. He wiggled them but there was nothing there to dance before his eyes. Nothing attached to those twitching, cauterized stumps at the base of his knuckles.

He then remembered his other hand. He jerked his left arm around from behind him and saw that this hand too, was different, quite different. Odd, even. His pointer finger and his thumb were no longer there. Gone. Poof.

"Jesus," he whispered. "Oh."

THE PREVIOUS EVENING

"Welcome to Kentucky, ladies and gentlemen. It's time to show you a bit of pride, something we're known for."

A neighing came from the shadows off to the left of the podium.

"Who doesn't love a strong, beautiful Kentucky Thoroughbred? The Bluegrass is known for it, y'all," the woman's voice twanged falsely. "Ponygirl on up here, Caerulean."

Into the light of the pedestal, led by a thick leather leash, was a startlingly beautiful blond-haired woman. She came on all fours, neighing and tossing her head back. The bright light caught her eyes and they appeared to burn with a violent blue.

"Caerulean," Jefferson whispered, "blue."

He reached into his jacket pocket, pulled out his bidding paddle but never took his eyes off Caerulean, the ponygirl.

He couldn't remember how high the bidding went. It didn't matter. He was good for it. Jefferson was not going to be outbid. He never lost. Never.

He took careful note of her entirety as she spun slowly before him. The crisp never-before-worn leather, not a scuff or mark on it, barely covering her ample but not overly large or small breasts. The horsetail protruding from the plug-hole in her leather bottoms. The mouthbit clamped between her straight white teeth. All of her.

When the gavel rapped onto the podium, he downed the last of his third, or maybe fourth, eighteen-year bourbon, and made his way out of the room. He left the way he'd come, entering the foyer of the sprawling, impressive house he'd never seen before.

He checked his tie and teeth in the mirror.

"Another, sir?"

A wafer-thin man stood a step and a half behind him proffering another glass, shining amber liquid seemingly as still as the water around Monet's ice floes.

Jefferson finished adjusting his tie before turning and taking the glass.

"Thank you," he said, sipping. "Where do I pick up my property?"

"It will be delivered to your room, sir."

"Good," Jefferson said. "Good."

He closed the door behind him and sighed in expectance. He felt giddy.

"Caerulean," he said aloud.

He walked over to the full-length mirror, casked in what must've been mahogany, and looked himself over. He toyed with his tie some more. He set the eighteen-year, the bourbon, on the tasteful desk and debated taking off the jacket or keeping it on. What kind of air did he want to give off? Did he want to seem personal and informal? It was custom tailored, the jacket, like everything else he wore, and fit him perfectly.

He stood still and gauged the temperature of the room. It was a bit warm for the jacket. He walked over to the

14

touchscreen thermostat and dropped it seven degrees. The air pulsed through the vents, both overhead and near the floors, instantly.

He smiled, picked the eighteen-year, the bourbon, up off the desk and sat down on the taut, freshly made bed to wait. He hadn't but just made the faintest crease in the thick down comforter when there was a gentle rapping at the door. A rush of butterflies spilled out into his stomach as he shot back to his feet.

He frowned.

That will not do, he thought. He would not be the excited twelve-year-old, child not bourbon, readying himself to open up his presents on Christmas morning. He made himself take a few deep, slow breaths, ignoring another set of tact raps, before leisurely making his way to the door, stopping in front of the mirror to adjust his tie again in the process.

Jefferson opened the door and there she was.

"Caerulean," he said, taking the proffered leash from the shadowhand.

He turned and pulled on the leash until it was taut. She looked up at him from the heavily carpeted hallway floor and some more butterflies knocked about in his stomach. Jefferson had the fleeting thought they weren't butterflies after all. They were moths battering an exposed light bulb, throwing themselves into it. Then he lost himself in his ponygirl's violently blue eyes and the heavy door clicked softly shut behind them.

NOW

Jefferson forced himself to stand, to look away from his maimed hands. He forced himself to squash any thought of more vomiting. There was nothing left to vomit. There was nothing he could do about his hands out here in the middle of nowhere. He had to find his way back to the house, back to his Mercedes, back to reality. He'd get himself to the University of Kentucky Medical Center and everything would be right as rain.

But where are my fingers?

He just knew, somehow, that he wouldn't find his fingers around him, where he woke up—came to, more like it. He half-assedly looked around him, careful not to move too quickly. He didn't find them.

"Fuck it," he huffed.

Breathing was hard, 'labored' they'd probably dub it when he got to the hospital. The hospital, society, a place with restraint, with sanity. He made his way up the path, the leaves glowing gold in the morning light, hoping to God he was heading back toward the house, the place of that out-of-hand party.

He shook his head and wished desperately, immediately

16

afterward, that he hadn't. The world spun and stuttered, a rebooting stream of some nature documentary. He spread his legs wide underneath him and let it pass. When it finally did, he saw the path.

THE PREVIOUS EVENING

"Good evening," he said.

His feet were spread a solid shoulder's width apart. He leaned back, slightly, so his waist was the closest part of him to her, Caerulean, his ponygirl.

She, still down on all fours, neighed softly, sultrily. It felt more like a purr to Jefferson. It got the hairs on the back of his arms and neck standing.

He just stood there over her for a minute, taking the sight of her in. He let her wait, down there on the floor, wait for his commands.

"Good," he said. "Good."

Then he began.

She was passive. She was so passive. He loved it. Jefferson felt a little taken aback at first because of her beauty, it was almost overbearing how beautiful she was, but he made it through. He started off slowly then moved right on ahead with his normal alacrity. He knew exactly what he wanted and he told her, down to the tiniest movement.

"Look up at me."

"Take it all."

"Stop using your hand."

"Neigh."

She was passive, so passive—at least at first.

He stood panting above her, shirt unbuttoned and fly still open. His crowning penis brushed against her cheek and a shiver ran up his spine. He turned his waist so it plopped into her other cheek then he rose to his tiptoes so it came to rest on her upturned forehead.

Jefferson began to get excited again.

He removed the shirt and began to do the same with his pants but stopped.

"Take them off," he told her.

Her eyes were so placid. They looked up without a shred of expectancy, no real sense of self or outrage or desire. Jefferson knew by the end of the night he'd change that. Her lips and mouth had been so dry he'd had to choke her with himself, hold her down despite the gag reflex, to get her wet.

He slowly pulled back from her, his penis sliding off her forehead and catching briefly on her plump, pink bottom lip. He took three steps back from her, leaned against the desk.

Keeping her eyes on his, she crawled the space in between them and pulled down his pants and boxers.

NOW

The path climbed, slowly but surely, up and up. He must've started off from the exact bottom of some valley. He had no conception of time. The sun seemed to hang obstinately where it did, not moving except to peek through the leaves to blind him. When he finally crested the ridge, he was sweat soaked and out of breath.

He turned back toward the way he'd come and saw nothing but lush rolling hills stretching out into the hazy, quickly warming morning. The sky was blue and cloudless. He turned back around and saw that the path widened and there, what looked to be miles ahead of him, the house where'd he'd bought and paid for Caerulean, his ponygirl.

"Jesus," he whispered.

He started his long walk back, his sensitive, bare feet already cut and bleeding.

THE PREVIOUS EVENING

He directed her to the bed. He had her remove the tail plug and became her tail.

"Pretend this is the fucking Derby," he told her.

She neighed and galloped while remaining stationary on the large bed. She did not cry out, not in agony or ecstasy or disgrace.

After he'd finished again, he collapsed onto the down comforter and closed his eyes. The smile on his face felt hot. A bit of sweat stung his left eye but he liked a little pain.

Good pain, he thought. *Everybody likes a little good pain. Pain so sweet it makes you ache.*

"Order us a bottle of that eighteen-year," he said, his eyes still shut.

He felt the bed move slightly, feeling the air conditioner brush lavishly across his eyelids, then listened as his ponygirl picked up the phone and made the call.

When the phone clicked gently back onto its base, Jefferson opened his eyes. The tray ceiling stepped up, seemingly in reverse, to a point some fifteen feet above the bed. The steps must've been nearly a foot each, laced with a trim work so intrinsic Jefferson didn't even have a guess as to how much it would've cost to include in every room of the place. At the exact center of the ceiling, when it finally reached its zenith and became a flat surface, there was a small red dot. Jefferson squinted his eyes trying to make it come in more clearly but couldn't. The ceiling was too far up.

There was a soft but quick rapping at the door. Jefferson lifted his head, tucking his forearms behind it, and watched Caerulean, still on all fours, make her way to the door. With the tail plug no longer in place, Jefferson watched her anus as she crawled. It seemed to him a dark, seeing eye, watchful and indolent. A little bit of jism shone under the yellow light.

When she made it to the door, she neighed softly and the door was opened from the other side. From the darkness of the hall a bottle was extended by a white-gloved hand. Caerulean sat back on her legs, the brown eye no longer watching Jefferson, and took the bottle. There was a nod of her beautiful blond head and the hand receded. The door was closed with a muted click.

Caerulean turned and made as if to rise, to carry the bottle back across the room to where he lay on the bed.

"No," he said. "On your back."

Her eyes remained vacuous. She dropped her left hand back to the floor and reached around, bottle in other hand, and sat it on her back. She fiddled with it momentarily, getting the balance just right, before setting her other hand onto the floor and carefully, very slowly, making her way to the bed.

"You better not drop it," he said.

Her eyes showed nothing.

"That's right. I'll have to really punish you if you do."

She made it. Somehow, she made it. Jefferson couldn't believe it. The bottle rode standing, like some jungle prince on a ceremonial elephant. It shifted this way, then that, with each of her movements but it did not fall.

22

"Yes," he said, pushing himself to the edge of the bed. "That's a good girl. Bring it here, honey."

She whickered softly but her expression showed nothing. Not concentration, not effort, nothing. She stopped just short of the bed and turned in a small half circle so her body acted as a table, presenting the unopened eighteen-year bourbon bottle, dripping with condensation that ran in rivulets down the well-defined curves on her back, to Jefferson.

"That's right," he said again.

He reached down, took up the bottle and held it above Caerulean's bare back. He shook the bottle so more droplets spattered down. The bottle was frigid to the touch and Jefferson mused that it must've been kept in a freezer for some time. With each drop, Jefferson waited for a flinch. His hand was burning with the cold of holding the bottle. Caerulean didn't flinch.

He crinkled up the foil and shifted the cork until he was able to remove it. It came out with a popping sound that reminded him of the tail plug he'd removed from his ponygirl. He smiled and told her to bring him his glass.

NOW

The woods hung over the path like outstretched arms, bayonets or bones. It felt like all three to Jefferson. Rays of light sliced through and stood ahead of him like sentinel lasers, some futuristic natural alarm system. His steps were ginger, his feet really smarting. He couldn't remember the last time he'd actually been barefoot, aside from the shower. He had a ninety-five dollar pair of Tuscan leather slippers he wore around the house.

Must've been six years old, he thought, *the last time I'd gone more than a half-dozen steps barefooted.*

He still couldn't make out the house from the forest. His head beat a dull drum of pain and dehydration. He felt as if his mouth had been forced full of cotton left there for hours before being removed, leaving his tongue mummified, foreign.

He made to cough and something rattled hard in his chest and he felt weak, dizzy for a moment. When it passed and he thought he was able to continue, he coughed again. He covered his mouth with the his closed stub of a fist. When he pulled it back he saw that it was speckled with blood. It looked obscene to him in the flittering sunlight, his blood on

24

his marred hand. His heart rate increased and he began to pant.

I need to get to a hospital, he thought. *Soon.*

"Jesus," he whispered. "What happened last night?"

THE PREVIOUS EVENING

He made her pour the drink.

"Three fingers," he told her. "I think I can fit more into you."

She made no response but to pour a perfect three fingers worth of bourbon into the glass. He took it from her outstretched hands and took a long pull.

He watched her watching him. It was a bit unnerving. There was no distrust in her eyes. Not the hint of expectancy. She was just there. On her knees, leaned back on her calves staring up at him on the edge of the bed.

He drained the rest of the glass. It was smooth but still bourbon, tears welled up in his eyes and a gasping "ah" worked its way up as the fiery liquid went down.

Caerulean didn't make to refill his glass. She didn't even ask if she could have a glass of her own.

"What to do with you?" he said. "What ever shall we do?"

He grinned but it felt forced.

He'd removed her costume bottoms with his teeth, the smell of the fresh leather heavy and enticing in his nostrils. Jefferson had decided it was time to delve into Caerulean's womanhood. To make his mark there. She hadn't responded the other two times, at the other two locations.

She'll respond now, he thought.

"Whinny," he said.

She whinnied. He picked her up in both of his arms. She was light and cold to the touch. He flung her onto the bed. She didn't struggle or fight. There were no awkward movements from her at all. The way she hit the bed and remained perfectly still in the same position brought an eerie image of a stone hitting the surface of a pond, disappearing under, but not changing the surface.

A wall of hate welled inside him.

"Bitch," he spat.

He lifted her chin with his left hand and open-handedly slapped her with his right.

Her blond hair jerked back with the force and the slap seemed to echo up into the high ceiling. Caerulean did not react. She remained exactly as she'd been moved to.

Jefferson jerked her chin upward and toward him again. He glared down into her expressionless face.

"Bitch."

He slapped her again. Then again. Then again.

NOW

The path ended at the foot of an expansive backyard leading up to the gigantic wraparound deck of the house. It loomed a story above the ground supported by thick, straight beams. There was a small fire pit with several chairs around it, an umbrellaed table and covered swing scattered like islands in the yard. The grass was cut, smelled like a freshly done job, and sharp under Jefferson's feet. He gritted his teeth and made for the stair set ascending to the deck.

When he passed the fire pit, he saw the thinnest trail of gray smoke snaking away from the charred wood. He held his hands above it and felt the heat in his fingers. Even the ones that were no longer there. His stomach dropped from somewhere within and he turned quickly away from the fire.

God, oh God, oh God, he thought.

There were several empty and half-empty bottles of beer and wine at the foot of the stairs. He grabbed a Stella Artois and drained it. He tossed it into the yard with a dull thud and picked up another, swishing the stale beer around in his mouth then spitting it out. The beer greatly upset his stomach—which quaked and rumbled but did not erupt, there wasn't anything left in there to dispel—but his mouth was so dry.

He picked up a bottle of Ovid Red, saw that nearly a quarter of it remained, and carried it with him as he climbed the stairs on his cut feet. The steps were dew-wet and cold. He leaned heavily on the railing for support, easing the burden on his feet.

He looked up at the house as he climbed. All the windows were closed and dark, shuttered or curtained. Nothing seemed to move within the house. He strained his ears listening for any movement, any signs of life, but silence sang loudly. Nothing but blood and static filled his head.

He stepped up from the last of the stairs and crouched onto the railing, fighting to regain his breath. His chest felt like a busted child's rattle, little metal balls escaping through the bent gaps in the wiring with each shake.

The deck was the picture of the morning after. Bottles and ashtrays were scattered on every surface, deck railing, tables, floor. The five sets of French doors leading into the house were closed and dark. Curtains hung limply in their panes.

Jefferson lifted the Ovid to his lips and drank.

He stared at the doors and drank again.

"Hello?" he said.

His voice sounded immense to him in the quiet.

"Hello?" he called again, more quietly.

He finished the bottle, turned and let it drop from his hands down onto the yard below. It did not shatter.

The door handle was all ice daggers, sending a wave of shivers across his body. He half-expected it to be locked but it wasn't. It turned silently, well-oiled, and opened into the darkness of a cavernous living room. He stepped up and in but stood there, just inside the door, straining against the darkness waiting for his eyes to adjust.

"Hello?" he said.

The room was heavy with silence. His eyes gradually began to adjust. He took several cautious steps inside.

"Hello? Anybody home?"

The carpet was soft and comforting. He knew he was probably leaving bloodstains all over it—it was a luscious thick, white shag, if he could recall properly—but he didn't care. He bumped into a coffee table, creating a ripple of clinking bottles to shatter the silence. He winced and couldn't help but feel that was something akin to farting at a funeral. The silence was that heavy, that funereal.

He made his way to the wall opposite the door he had come in and flicked the light switch. Nothing happened. He flipped the switch up and down several times but there was no light to be had.

"Great," he said.

The sprawling couches looked like sleeping beasts in the darkness of their den. He could make out shapes, lumps on the couches, but nothing more than that really. It was too dark.

"Hello," he said again, louder. "Hey. Wake up."

The lumps did not move.

I know the feeling, Jefferson thought. His head still buzzed with the hangover.

He walked across the room to the covered windows and threw back the curtains. The bright light streaked across the room and, his vision having finally acclimated to the darkness, he had to shield his eyes from the luminance.

He expected groans of foggy pain and anger from the lumps on the couches. There was no sound.

"Hey, wake up."

He had to keep his eyes squinted in the glare.

"C'mon. I've got to get to a doctor. I'm hurt."

He walked to the couches. With each step, he saw more clearly that the lumps on the couches were indeed people.

There were two on the couch nearest him, sprawled across each other as if instantly asleep when they threw themselves down. There were four others on the even larger couch against the wall on the other side of the room.

"Oh, God," Jefferson whispered.

The people on the couch were not going to wake up. They would not help him get to a doctor.

"Oh, God."

The woman's black skirt was pasty with congealed blood. Her thin—what appeared to be silk—blouse was askew, her breasts exposed in the morning light. Her eyes were wide but empty, seeing nothing. Her nose was gone, simply no longer there. In its place was a gaping hole, black and red filled, yawning up toward Jefferson.

Beside her on the couch was another woman. This one naked with the exception of a leather gag across her mouth and rough looking rope binding her hands and ankles. Her eyes were also wide and unseeing.

Dead. Both of these women are dead.

"Oh, Jesus."

Jefferson spun on his heels and ran to the other couch. Four dead men. One had obviously been stabbed to death. He couldn't bring himself to study the others.

Jefferson's mind raced but got nowhere. He plopped down onto the thick carpeting and held his face in his stubbed hands.

PREVIOUSLY

"Hey, Jeffy."

Jefferson looked up from his monitor. Richard stood in the doorway to Jefferson's office.

"What's up?"

"Man, there's a par-tay happening this weekend. I mean this one is supposed to be the real deal."

"Oh, yeah?"

"Yeah. Crazy," Richard said, stepping inside the office and pulling the door closed behind him.

Jefferson sat back in his chair and rubbed his eyes. He'd been going through this briefing for the better part of an hour and had a little tension headache in the works from staring at the screen.

Richard pulled one of the thin metal, modernistic chairs around the desk and sat facing Jefferson.

"They're gonna have it all, man. Sex-slave auction. You can bid and buy whatever you want. Anything."

Jefferson wiped the eye goo from his hands on his pants.

"An auction?"

"Yeah. You in?"

Jefferson hesitated.

"It's not going to be like that time in Murray, is it?"

Richard's face darkened.

"You know that wasn't my fault. I thought they'd been there before. She put up such a good front."

"Yeah. Everything she knew came right out of that *Shades of Grey* shit."

Richard made a disgusted huff.

"And if my memory serves me well, I think you had to settle that out of court . . ." Jefferson let the sentence trail off.

"Jesus, this is different, Jeffy. These people are professionals. You have to complete the paperwork before you can even be officially invited."

"Paperwork?"

Richard nodded and reached into an inside pocket of his suit jacket. He brought out a set of papers, stapled and folded hot-dog style and passed them over to Jefferson.

"Waiver of responsibility and criminal background check."

Jefferson lifted his eyebrows and unfolded the document. The paper was thick, expensive. At the top of each page was a raised letterhead indicating the documents had come from *Bad Pain Entertainment*.

"Bad pain, huh?" Jefferson said.

Richard grinned and nodded enthusiastically.

Jefferson skimmed through the paperwork. It did, indeed, seem like the real deal to him. His eyes widened slightly at this sentence: "Auction winners' purchase must be paid in full at the time of purchase and services purchased will be delivered and performed without supervision upon purchase."

"They've definitely crossed all the 't's and dotted all the 'i's," he said, refolding the paperwork and handing it back to Richard.

"I told you, man. They're professionals."

Richard shook his head and didn't take the document.

"Those're for you. If you're in, I mean. I'm definitely going. I'm hellbent on some more needleplay. Domm Monica's was the hottest shit I've ever had."

"You and your erotic acupuncture," Jefferson said in his best old patronizing woman voice. "Kids these days."

"Ok, Mr. Barnyard-Animal-Sex," Richard quipped.

They laughed.

NOW

Time passed. When Jefferson regained control of himself the sun was in a different place. The light coming through the windows changed. The bodies on the couches remained.

I gotta get out of here.

"Keys," he said.

The keys to his Mercedes AMG C63 coupe were in his room on the third floor.

Jefferson rose on shaking legs and left the room, doing his best to keep his eyes on the floor before him. He didn't think he could stand to look at the bodies again.

At the entrance to the hallway, he passed a small table, a phone and hydrangea sitting on top. He scooped up the receiver and tapped 911. There were no button noises. The faceplate didn't illuminate the numbers he dialed. He put the phone to his ear knowing he wouldn't hear a dial tone, hope fluttering in his chest anyway.

Nothing came through the little speaker of the phone. Jefferson's chest seemed to pull within itself and tears pushed their way up with an overwhelming pressure. He slammed the phone onto the table and entered the hallway. With each step, he felt the thudding of his heartbeat and pulse.

He hadn't recognized any of the people from the living room but couldn't stop seeing their faces peering sightlessly out of the shadows at him.

What happened in there?

It couldn't have been an accident. Everyone in there had been dead and each looked like they had died in their own separate way. In the news, you could always count on an accidental death from rough play. The vanilla reporter telling the "grisly tale of a good time gone bad" or some such nonsense.

But this . . .

Jefferson didn't know what this was. He didn't know why he had awakened in the woods missing fingers. He didn't know why there were six dead people in the living room. He didn't know why the house was without power. He didn't know and wished desperately he'd never submitted the paperwork to attend this party.

The hallway was dark. There were no windows. He kept the outside of his hand trailing across the wall—careful to avoid catching the stub on anything—as he made his way toward the end of the hall, where the staircase ascended to the second and third floors. The flooring was not carpeted. It was an old, well-polished hardwood. It creaked under his sore, bare feet seemingly every other step.

There was a foreignness to the hallway in the dark. It felt foreboding. Sullen and waiting. Behind each closed door, he felt the looming presence of some murderous anger waiting to barge out and take him. He'd never felt this scared in his life. His mouth felt metallic now. He wasn't sure whether that was better or worse than the cotton-stuffed feeling from earlier.

What is happening? What is happening?

THE PREVIOUS EVENING

"I'll meet you there. I'm behind on the Oliver deal. Got a few things to finish up and I'll see you there."

Jefferson sighed into the phone.

"You have the address. Quit being a little bitch. You can go to the dance on your own, little Jeffy."

"All right. See you there," Jefferson said, ending the call.

He went back into the bathroom and looked at himself in the mirror. He ran careful fingers through his gelled hair, getting it just right. He ran through the rest of his appearance: checking his nose, his teeth, his tie, his freshly ironed shirt tucked straightly into the freshly ironed pants.

He nodded at himself in the mirror and smiled.

"Ponygirl, ponygirl," he sang softly. "Gonna find me a ponygirl tonight."

He punched the address into the car's GPS.

"Jesus," he said. "That's way out in the middle of nowhere."

Three and a half hours, the drive would take. He pushed the car out onto 27 heading toward Interstate 64. The engine purred, responsive to even the smallest flutter of his foot. He weaved through traffic and bolted out onto the interstate.

He kept the windows up despite the comfort of the evening. He adjusted the climate and radio until he was satisfied. He let the headlights shine out in front of him and his mind unwind. He kept imagining how it would play out. He would get his ponygirl. If there was a cow that was hot enough, he'd just have her change. He wasn't fucking some cow. He was going to fuck a ponygirl.

His pants contracted and relaxed as he went through the debauchery he had in store for his ponygirl. He didn't bring anything, the paperwork said all would be supplied with the purchase, but he knew he wanted his pony collared and without hard limits. He'd been under a lot of stress lately. He wanted to shake it off and let loose. He wanted to see how far he was willing to go. He wanted to hurt his ponygirl, really hurt her. Watch her writhe in pain and pleasure until she begged him to stop or continue or, better yet, both at the same time.

He tried Richard on his cell from somewhere on the midnight Mountain Parkway, rolling hills and blue-black trees under a skeleton moon. His call went straight to voicemail. Jefferson hesitated for a moment but decided to leave one. Jefferson waited through Richard's recorded voice telling him to leave a message with his name, number and "case number or project name if applicable after the tone" and, after the beep sounded through the speaker, said, "Here's to no Dungeon Monitors, Rich. Let's have a ball."

He ended the call and felt his penis hard and hot against his inner thigh.

There was no one on the road ahead of him or behind him. He let his foot ease the pedal closer to the floor. The white lines began to blur on the black pavement.

A matte black mailbox marked the drive. He turned in and

the gravel crunched and pinged under the wheels. He had to control himself, ease the car down or the bumpy drive would rattle the fillings from his teeth. Being this close to the party, this close to another night of absolute control sparked him in ways nothing else did. He took a deep breath, held it and purposely took his foot off the gas pedal until the car slowed to a crawl.

The drive twisted and turned, a narrow parting of the forest surrounding it, really. It took him nearly fifteen minutes to reach the house. The forest abruptly came to an end and the mansion stood there, waiting.

There were other cars in the u-shaped drive, which looked freshly paved, reflecting the light of the moon back dully in the night. He pulled in behind a Rolls, chuckling to himself. Some people didn't know restraint.

He didn't see the man approach the car. Didn't hear any sign of the man presenting himself. When Jefferson opened the door and made to step out onto the asphalt he was just standing there, drink in hand.

"Sir," the man said, offering the glass.

Jefferson took it and nodded.

He did his best not to show how spooked the man's appearance had made him. He'd been checking his teeth and hair in the mirror before he got out.

"This way, sir," the man said after Jefferson had shut his door.

He followed the bland little man up the stone stairs, through the open and waiting oak doors.

Servant. The word came into his mind like the artist of some song you've had stuck in your head for days. *This man is a servant. Doorman. Waiting to lead people inside.*

The foyer was impressive. Jefferson found himself slowing to look up at the high vaulted ceiling and the lavishly framed oil landscapes on the walls.

"This way, sir," the man called.

Even his voice is non-distinct. Nothing even remotely identifying about it. Just another voice.

The servant turned a corner, leading Jefferson into a long hallway.

This house is immense. This is going to be some party.

The servant slowed as if sensing Jefferson's excitement.

"We're going up to the office first, to take care of the accounts billing processing then I'll lead you to the auction block, sir."

Jefferson nodded.

Auction block. Jesus.

The room was the size of a three-car garage. It had high arching ceilings with bald, unfixtured lights hanging like nooses just a few inches above Jefferson's head. A wall of monitors showed people milling about at a cocktail party. Everyone dressed to the nines, all in black or dark colors. There was a grim satisfaction and excitement on their faces.

At the foot of the wall of monitors was a thick metallic desk. Behind it sat a woman smiling demurely up at Jefferson as he entered.

"Mr. Wellman, good evening," the woman said.

Her voice was harsh, in stark contrast with the softness of her face and lips. Her hair was buzzed down nearly to the scalp but it was becoming on her. Jefferson normally didn't approve of the whole short hair on girls look but this woman, she pulled it off.

"Good evening," Jefferson said, smiling.

"Please have a seat."

The servant unfolded a metal chair and sat it just behind Jefferson.

Jefferson thanked the servant with a curt nod and took a seat. He crossed his right leg over his left thigh and cupped both of his hands around his shin.

"I'm glad you've decided to join us tonight, Mr. Wellman."

Jefferson nodded.

"You haven't missed anything, don't worry. The auction hasn't opened, just a little meet and greet is happening currently."

Her smile didn't seem to touch her eyes. Or at least not in the way her face presented the smile. Jefferson thought the eyes radiated a harder smile, one that should curve the lips more, show more teeth.

"We just need to get some billing information from you before we can allow you to bid."

Jefferson nodded, doing his best to look nonplused, a trifle annoyed at the thought of talking about something as trivial as finances.

"Do you want to withdraw directly from your banking account or place all purchases on a credit card?"

Jefferson sighed, sniffed then shifted on the uncomfortable metal chair to retrieve his thick wallet.

"Or if you'd like, there are others ways of paying," she said, leaning forward in her chair. She placed her elbows on the desk and clasped her hands together.

Jefferson saw she was missing the index finger on her left hand. He did his best not to draw attention to his noticing of this fact. He let his wallet sit on his lap and resumed his former position in the uncomfortable chair.

"What do you mean?" he asked.

"Well, some of our clients, for various reasons, do not want any charge from our organization showing up on their account statements—checking, credit or otherwise. They have spouses, occupations, high positions in society that warrant protections against knowledge of these sort of gatherings coming to light, you see."

"I see," Jefferson said slowly.

"Good."

They looked at each other for a moment in silence. Flickers of light from several of the monitors of the party behind the woman caught Jefferson's attention.

"It's almost time to begin," the woman said, not taking her eyes from Jefferson's.

Jefferson tightened his grip on his shin.

This bitch better not make me miss out on my ponygirl.

"Perhaps we can work something out later? I see you're antsy to get to the bidding, and I don't blame you. Tonight's product is top-flight, Mr. Wellman, as you're soon to see. I trust you have the means to pay for anything you're willing to purchase?"

"Of course, of course," Jefferson said, the lights in the main room, what must be the room in which the auction was to take place, flashing twice more.

"Good," she said. "Happy bidding."

It took a show of real restraint for Jefferson to not push and prod the servant to lead him more quickly down the long hall. If he'd known the way to the auction room—the auction block, it'd been called—he would have muscled his way around the nondescript man as soon as the door was shut behind him.

He checked his breathing and, annoyingly, found he had begun to sweat a little bit. He reached into his inner pocket for his handkerchief and dabbed at his forehead and temples.

"I can take that jacket for you, sir."

The man hadn't even turned around.

How did he know I was sweating? Jefferson wondered.

He looked ahead for a mirror or a window that would've reflected him forward to the servant but he didn't see one.

"No, no."

The jacket brought the look together. Jefferson chided himself on his inability to control himself and made a point to slow his stride a bit and breathe more evenly. He decided he would will himself to stop this nervous and excited sweating. He wouldn't go throwing his appearance off because he wasn't able to control himself. That wouldn't do.

"This way, sir."

The servant rounded a corner at the end of the hall, opened a double-set of thick oak doors and disappeared amongst the party goers.

Jefferson blinked into the gloominess of the room. The monitors back in the room at the end of the hallway had made it seem bright and festive. He stood there, taking stock of the room through his slowly adjusting eyes. He looked for Richard but couldn't make him out in the crowd.

The lights of the room blinked again and everyone began to end their conversations and seek out seats. Windows running nearly the length of the room's front wall and showing the faceless white moon and unblinking stars backed a small podium.

Jefferson watched the partygoers find their seats. All seemed to know exactly where they were going. Jefferson hated the woman for making him late. Had he been ushered straight into the room he would've found his seat long ago and known where to go instead of standing just inside the door looking like as obvious as vanilla.

"Bitch," Jefferson whispered.

"This way, sir."

The little man stood just to the left of him. Jefferson hadn't seen him approach.

Jefferson nodded, once, curtly and followed the man through the aisle to his seat, two rows back from the podium.

A little placard sat on his seat.

Reserved for Mr. Jefferson Wellman, Esq.

Jefferson smiled, plucked up the card and sat.

A bright light above the podium flashed once, the dim lighting of the room was extinguished and the auction began.

NOW

Jefferson made it to the end of the hall. The stair set leading up the two flights of stairs to his room sat behind the closed door to the left. The door directly in front of him, his hand resting just to the right of the knob, was the room where he'd met with the woman. The room with the monitors.

Little flickering images of televised murders flashed in his mind. He saw the bodies on the couches alive, saw them butchered from the perspective of small nondescript cameras hidden carefully in the corners of the room.

He moved his hand to the knob but found it shaking uncontrollably.

"Hello," he croaked.

There was no sound from within the room.

"Is there anybody in there? Please. Help."

The last little vestiges of bravado—Jefferson realized as he heard his own voice—rested in not succumbing to panic. He heard the shakiness, the horror, the desperation in his voice and knew he was only barely, just barely, in control of himself. The skin on his body felt ready to tear free and go sprinting back down the hall out the front door, down the drive and away into the mountain morning.

Jefferson forced himself to clear his throat and try again.

"Hello," he called, his voice two shades deeper than it normally was. "There are people hurt. They need help."

He turned his hand on its side and beat a firm drum on the door.

"Open up."

He felt his knees meet and knew they were knocking.

Jesusgod, pull it together, he told himself.

Nothing from within the room. He stilled himself and tried the doorknob, slapping his hand on it and twisting madly, much how he had removed Band-Aids when he was a kid—as quickly as possible before any chickening out could occur.

It was locked.

He backed away from the door, expecting it to burst open any moment. The fact that it had been locked seemed supremely sinister to Jefferson. He backed toward the door leading to the stairs without taking his eyes from it.

He turned the knob to that one and found it, thankfully, unlocked. He plunged into the darkness of the windowless stairwell, pulling the door closed behind him.

He stood there wide-eyed and unseeing in the darkness, his back against the door, his own breathing beating a hammer in his ears. Sweat stung his eyes. His nostrils felt clogged and bloody. He could hear the faint whistling of the air he sucked through his teeth.

Nobody had come out of the monitor room.

He squeezed his eyes shut and took in a long pull of air, holding it until little stars flashed in front of him. Then he let it out in a steady push.

"OK," he whispered. "OK."

He opened his eyes, not surprised, just dismayed he couldn't see anything. He'd have to ascend two flights of stairs completely blind. He reached out into the darkness for the railing he knew was somewhere before him. He took stut-

46

tering, faltering inchworm steps forward. He felt the slowing of time all the blind must feel. The hush of seconds into minutes.

He reached and came up empty. He regretted leaving the safety of the door to his back.

Should've scooted along the wall until I came on the stairs that way.

Irritated at himself, he lifted his left leg to take a normal step forward. He made to step down and fell forward, his foot catching on the first stair. He flung his diminished hands forward and barely caught himself from falling flat on his face. His nubbed fingers screamed in pain.

"Shit!"

He shifted the weight to his forearms and pushed himself to a shaky stance, somewhere between kneeling and standing. He reached blindly for the railing and, eventually—after what felt like hours—found it.

The climb was slow. Each step, unsteady and nerve-racking. Jefferson made it up the first flight of stairs and saw a sliver of light peeking out from under the door to the second floor. It was a thin shaft of light but compared to the complete blackness of the stairwell it was vivid. He stood on the landing debating on whether or not he should try the door to the second floor.

Maybe there's somebody alive that can help, he thought. *Or, maybe, there's more dead there too. Maybe the door is locked and wouldn't that just be terrifying in itself?*

He didn't try the door. He scooted across the landing until the next set of stairs started. He wished he could see, wished the lights were working. The light from under the door did next to nothing to illuminate his path.

Halfway up he heard the noise. It was a low noise, something made far back in the throat, not quite a choking but close. He stood as still as his shaking body would allow and put everything he had into listening.

"Hello?" he called after a moment. "Is anyone there?"

The noise did not intensify or diminish, it persisted.

It's definitely coming from upstairs, he thought.

He took another step up and listened. Then another and another until he was on the next landing. He scooted his feet in wide, quaking arcs around him. Searching for the source of the noise.

"Hello?"

The noise persisted and Jefferson determined it came from the next landing, the one to the third floor, to his room. The noise was louder now. Jefferson was closer. It was something akin to a moan and a choke. He'd made similar noises on several occasions. He loved being choked out by his women just prior to orgasm. When you finally came, with all that oxygen deprivation, it was the most intense eruption of your life, every single time. Despite himself, he grew stiff.

"Hello?" he called up, craning his neck and slitting his eyes to see up the final flight.

There was no response. Just the noise and surrounding silence.

Jefferson mounted the first stair, keeping his eyes up and scanning.

Then he heard the footsteps. They sounded like boots made completely out of rock, thudding down the third floor hall.

THUD THUD THUD THUD

Oh, Jesus! his mind screamed.

The steps were approaching the door to the stairwell.

Jefferson turned and scampered down the stairs.

The killer's coming. He's going to kill me.

Jefferson stumbled toward the wall, misjudged his location and fell headlong down the stairs he'd just ascended. He smacked onto the stairs somewhere halfway down, feeling something snap in his shoulder.

He rolled forward, his feet flipping over his head and sending a sickening wave of dizziness washing over him. He crumpled onto the landing in the thin shaft of light coming from under the second story door.

He scooted himself back against the door just in time to see a pillar of light flash into being on the stairway wall above him as the third floor door was opened. The light yawned until it took up nearly the entirety of the wall above him. A shape stepped out into the light, a great shadow person looming above.

Oh God.

Dust mites danced in the fully blossomed light. They floated around the shape giving it a fiery appearance. A fire burned so hot it was black, shedding flickering flames like dandruff.

The shadow stood tall, still for a moment. The smooth oval shape of its head turned slightly and a more defined profile of the shape came into being in the pillar of light. Jefferson held his breath. Then the shape shot forward and halved in size. The noise from the landing above erupted in a frenzy of struggle.

Jefferson pulled himself up and yanked the door open and shot through, running the fastest he'd ever run in his life down the dim second story hallway.

THE PREVIOUS EVENING

"Another," he said.

He heard his voice for what it was: satisfied, satiated. The comforter lay loosely over him. He had his hands under the feather pillow behind his head. His breathing was slow, steady, relaxed.

Caerulean got up from the bed, red welts whelping up across her back, butt and thighs. She did not limp to the desk and the bottle of the eighteen-year, the bourbon. No, she took the steps with surety and ease.

Jefferson frowned.

He wanted a cigar and, maybe, something else. Something that would give him a little more edge, more vigor.

He watched her uncork the bottle and pour another three fingers of bourbon into his glass. Her hands were steady, her motions economical. She corked the bottle and brought him the drink.

He let her hold it there, arm extended, face blank, while he slowly—taking his time about it—moved the pillows behind him against the rich headboard. He beat them softly, getting them just right, then eased himself against them in a sitting position, his penis coming out from under the cover of the down comforter.

He took the glass.

Caerulean let her arm fall back at her side and stood there beside the bed, completely naked, smooth faced and blank-eyed.

Jefferson frowned and sipped the bourbon, the eighteen-year.

"I need something," he told her.

She didn't reply.

"I was under the impression that this was a party in which things can be gotten."

Nothing about her countenance said she was even listening. A flicker of rage leapt through his chest. He held it at bay, for the moment.

"I want some cocaine," he said.

He chided himself at the juvenile sense of deviancy he felt at saying the words. After what he'd just had this girl—his ponygirl—do, wanting drugs seemed sophomoric at best.

Caerulean turned on her heels and went back to the desk. She picked up the phone and punched in a few numbers.

"Yes," she said into the phone. Her voice was harsh yet quiet. "Yes."

There was a pause while somebody from the other line spoke into the phone.

Jefferson tried to watch her face but his eyes wandered on down to the rest of her. He felt the stirring of desire and knew the cocaine would make this a very long evening for his little ponygirl.

Yes, indeed.

He had her on her knees at the foot of the bed, taking him in slow laps, when there was a knock at the door. Jefferson flicked his head toward the door and Caerulean made to get up.

"No," he told her. "On your knees."

Her face didn't change.

I'll change that, he thought. *You better damn well believe I'll get something from you, my little ponygirl.*

He watched her crawl across the room to the door on all fours. Her tight ass bounced with her sure motions, as did her breasts.

Jefferson reached over to the nightstand and took up the bourbon. He finished the glass and turned back to the door.

Caerulean was crawling back across the room with a little plastic baggie of white powder clenched between her teeth. Her eyes were on him but there was nothing there. No emotion, no worry, no concern. No desire for the high she had nestled between her perfectly straight, white teeth.

He was still hard. He stood up from the bed, above her. He looked down at her, seeing the pulse in his penis pulsing like the light in a lighthouse. Jefferson moved himself so he could flick the bag dangling from her mouth back and forth.

"Yes," he said. "Yes."

He made her line it up, right there on the desk with the pad of Bad Pain stationery. Quarter-inch lines of some of the whitest white he'd ever seen.

He shook with anticipation.

"Get my wallet," he told her. "From my pants."

His gaze shot from the four lines he had his ponygirl make for him to the ponygirl herself crawling, ass up, over to his crumpled pants by the bed. He watched her take out the wallet and put it between her teeth and crawl back to where he stood, naked, shaking and hard.

He took the wallet from her mouth and riffled through the bills for a hundred. He pulled it out slowly from his wallet, going out of his way to flash the others just like it. Then he let the wallet flop to the floor and rolled up the bill.

He felt the smile spread across his face, the hair on the back of his neck and thighs pull the skin tight.

"Oh, yes," he whispered, bending over the table and putting the hundred-dollar straw in place. "Oh, yes."

Things blurred together, sped up. He got sloppy and aggressive. He remembered feeling distinctly like a cat, ears slicked back, eyes wide with a playful menace. Playful for the cat only. The mouse was not an equal party to the game.

He got her to call for the whips. The straps and chains. The gag.

On and on and on. Loving every second of it. The seconds seeming less than seconds than fractions of blinks.

I will make it count, he remembered thinking. *I will make you hurt. I will hurt you. Yes.*

But he remembered the eyes of his ponygirl, his Caerulean. Blank, unfeeling, unimpressed.

He had her do the most despicable things he could come up with. He wanted her humiliated. He wanted her teary eyed, snot nosed, begging for mercy. He wanted her moaning, no, *screaming* in the throes of a most violent, painful ecstasy. He needed it. He needed her to need it.

He had her naked in the bathtub. The water off. He stepped up onto the rim of the tub on his unsteady legs.

"Hold me," he demanded.

Her hands went up around his hips, her thumbs on his hip bone, her fingers digging into his ass cheeks. Then he pissed on her. It was a thick stream of vile yellow. He used his hand to aim it directly into her face.

When her eyes and mouth shut, a flinching natural reaction to being splashed, a surge of pride filled him.

"Open them."

She opened her mouth and he watched the piss beat off her perfect teeth and pink tongue, spilling out onto her pouty lips. Little beads of yellow splashed onto his legs and stomach, his feet.

"Open them," he barked.

Her eyes squeezed open but only fractionally. They blinked shut every time he tried to piss in them. He felt her fingers dig deeper into his flesh.

Yes, he thought. *Yes. Feel it. Feel me.*

When he'd pissed all he could piss, he had her lick him clean. He had her start with his feet and work her way up to his stomach. He made sure she didn't miss an inch of his skin.

Then he had her shower. He pulled back the shower curtain and sat on the toilet. She stood under the ice cold water—he turned it on and, much to his chagrin, she didn't try to turn the handle—with her eyes open and blank. He had to tell her to use the soap. He had to tell her again to use the shampoo then the conditioner.

When she'd finished, he turned the shower off and made her stand, dripping and covered in gooseflesh under the air conditioner vent. He watched her shaking and smiled. Her face showed nothing but her body betrayed her.

She feels it. Yes, she does.

NOW

The hall came to a crossroads. It went straight, off into the darkness, to his left or, ahead, came to an end at a window and two more room doors.

Jefferson stood panting, hearing his pulse, feeling something rattling around in his lungs, looking down the long hallway to his left, not seeing an end. It was too dark. It could end just where the darkness blurred or it could keep going. He couldn't tell.

He turned around and stared down the hall in which he'd just run.

Nobody was behind him.

Not yet, he thought.

He started, at a laboring jog, down the long, dark hall.

There must be another set of stairs on this side of the house. There has to be.

Jefferson's chest beat erratically, flights of dizziness sweeping through him, forcing him to slow and, twice, stop completely. He wiped the cold, clammy sweat from his forehead with the back of his right hand. Sweat stung the wounds where his ring and pinky fingers were.

The hall darkened as it went. The sole lighting coming from one window he passed a couple dozen or more steps back. He slowed his pace and shot wary glances over his shoulder. Nobody appeared to be following him, at least not that he could tell.

What is going on?

He could finally see the end of the hall. He squinted into the darkness, trying to make it out more clearly. There was a door to the left. It was ajar.

Black as night in there.

Jefferson hoped it was another staircase, thought it was a good sign it was as dark as the other.

He pushed open the door slowly. It creaked slightly on its hinges but opened smoothly.

"Hello?"

There was no answer. He stepped through the door. He stood still and listened and, hearing nothing, moved to his right, feeling his way by the wall. The flooring under his sore feet was carpeting. He did his best not to dwell on this fact or the fact that the other staircase hadn't been carpeted.

The walls were smooth to the touch, cold. He moved slowly, carefully along the wall.

Should've reached the stairs by now, he thought.

His hand met something even colder than the wall. It gave with his motion and jingled.

A chain.

"What the—"

His chest met with something large. Jefferson scampered backward, lost his balance and tumbled onto his back, smacking the back of his head on the carpeted floor. He couldn't catch his breath. His head swam and he felt nauseous.

"Who's there?" he managed through a constricted whisper.

There was no reply.

Jefferson listened to the chains clanking together. He could hear something large swaying with them.

"Who's there?"

Jefferson scrambled to his feet and started backing away.

The room was too dark to make anything out.

"Stay away from me."

Jefferson bumped into the door, closing it and sending the room into utter darkness. He turned around and clawed at the door and, at first, couldn't find the doorknob. He panicked, screaming for help and slapping the closed door with the palms of his hands. Then he found the knob and pulled the door open.

He lunged from the room, tripped and fell on his hands and knees just outside the door. He crawled to the wall opposite, turned around and sat there panting, his back against the cool, rich wooden surface.

The door bounced off its stop on the inside wall and slowly began to shut again. As the door made its way to closure, Jefferson saw the faint outline of a person, wrapped in chains. The chains seemed to run the length of the room, strung from both the floor and the ceiling. The person's head was slumped forward, lolling on its chest. It appeared to be a man but the darkness made it hard to tell. No real concrete details could be distinguished. The man's feet did not touch the ground. He was completely suspended by the chains.

"Oh," Jefferson said.

As the door blocked the man from Jefferson's vision, he could make out a little more clearly that the man's arms were suspended outward from his shoulders, the slagging arms of a T. The limp arms of a deceased Jesus on the cross.

"Hey," he called. "Hey."

The door came to rest, not closed, but ajar.

He didn't know what to do.

Is he alive? Should I go in there and check on him?

Jefferson sat there running what was left of his fingers through his sweat matted hair. The strange mixture of his expensive hair gel and his unwashed hair and body wafted into his nostrils.

He looked back down the hallway, the way he'd come, and didn't see anybody, no pursuer.

He rocked his head back against the wooden wall several times, each one a little harder than the last. When he felt his brain jarring around in his skull, he stopped.

Think, Jefferson. What to do? How do I get out of this?

He stood, pushing himself up off the wall.

That man is probably dead. Nothing I can do for him.

Jefferson turned away from the partly open door and started walking back the way he'd come. His steps were short, staccato. He was ready to turn and run if whoever was in that staircase appeared before him. He didn't know where'd he'd run to but he'd run.

He made it back down the hall to the window. He looked out.

A gentle breeze rippled through the rolling tree tops of the mansion's backyard. There were no longer any smoke trails from the firepit near the path through the woods. The sun was blazing high in the cloudless sky. Any other day and it would've been beautiful. Today, though, it just seemed like a sick joke to Jefferson. Mocking.

He turned away from the window and continued on, back toward whatever awaited him upstairs.

THE PREVIOUS EVENING

Every time time tried to catch back up, Jefferson did another line.

"Lay down," he told Caerulean. "On your back."

She made to move toward the bed but he stopped her.

"On the floor."

She did as he asked, her face enragingly expressionless.

Jefferson took the little baggie, nearly empty, and dropped roughly to his knees on her stomach. He felt her breath rush out and her flat stomach muscles contract. She made no sound other than a slight "ugh" as the air in her lungs was forced out.

He smiled then, one by one, removed his knees from her stomach and placed them on the carpet beside her. He knelt forward, as if prostrating himself to pray. He carefully tilted the little plastic baggie until some of the powder spilled onto her stomach. He adjusted his aim and filled his ponygirl's shallow navel.

"Yes," he laughed. "Yes."

She lifted her head to see what he was doing.

"Don't you move, girl."

She set her head back on the floor. Her arms lay at her

side. He picked up her left and moved her hand to his penis. He wrapped her fingers around himself and started slowly going through the motions.

Caerulean began to move her arm, assisting with the act.

"No," Jefferson barked. "Don't you move, bitch."

Her hand went limp in his but he kept it clasped and moving.

He poured the rest of the baggie into her bellybutton then tossed it aside. He licked the powder that hadn't made it inside its natural cup, slowly, sloppily. He smacked his lips together and closed his eyes.

Then he picked up his pace, knelt low and finished the cocaine.

Things disappeared between realities. Time and space seemed to part, allowing Jefferson, his ponygirl there at his every beck and call, to slip in between and go for hours that only could've lasted seconds. His engine was running full throttle. He held nothing back. He used all the toys. Inserted himself and the toys wherever the fancy struck him. He reached four of his fingers into her mouth and stretched until he saw the corners of her lips crack then tear.

He laughed, cried, hooted and hollered. His last fleeting thought—desire, really—was the need to completely embarrass this ponygirl. This girl, seemingly made of stone, expressionless, unfeeling, must be made to sob, to scream for forgiveness, mercy.

Then the lights went out and he couldn't see or remember anything clearly.

NOW

He poked his head around the corner and saw no one. He made his way back to the door and turned the knob as slowly and quietly as he could. He pushed it in and listened.

The noise, the low moaning or whatever it had been, was gone. In its place was a heavy stillness, so quiet it screamed out portentously to Jefferson. It seemed pregnant with harm, danger.

I have no choice, he told himself.

He pushed the door open and slipped through. He moved as quickly as he could, figuring it gave him less of a chance of chickening out. He scooted along until he found the first stair, mounted it, and ascended.

He came to the first landing and listened.

Nothing but the screaming silence.

He found the railing and started up. He felt lightheaded but gritted his teeth against it. He ground and ground them together until he was sure he was flattening the tops of them together. Then he started chewing on the inside of his lips. Blood, coppery and metallic, filled his mouth.

He went to step up and there was nothing there. He'd reached the top of the stairs.

He found the wall and slowly made his way to the next wall then over to the door. He found the knob and opened the door. Bright, blinding light filled his eyes. He thought of hunting trips he'd taken, killing deer from the back of his uncle's four-by-four using a gigantic spotlight.

He stepped back, shielding his eyes and his foot met with something. He fell.

As the door shut itself, Jefferson saw what he'd tripped over. A naked man, completely gagged, wide-eyed and staring.

"Jesus," he gasped.

He scooted back and nearly tumbled back down the stairs, catching himself at the last moment on the railing.

"Jesus," he said again. "Are you OK?"

There was no answer. Jefferson knew there wouldn't be.

He sat there panting and panic-stricken in the dark.

"Are you OK?"

His voice broke and he began to weep.

Pull yourself together, man. Pull yourself together. You have to get out of here. You have to get the fuck out of here.

His own voice in his head. His words, the tenor of his voice, every bit the lawyer. Every bit the commanding leader. The slick suited man in control. Striding across the courtroom to meet with the judge, talk golf, politics, his case already won before it was even argued.

It was his own voice that brought Jefferson down from the ledge.

Stand up, goddamn it. Stand the fuck up, walk over to that door—don't you even think about tripping over that dead schmuck—and go get your fucking car keys.

Jefferson did as he was told. He toed his way to the dead man, poking him twice with his left foot then stepped over him and found the door. He braced himself for the blinding light of day and pulled the door open.

He stepped out into the hallway and let the door close behind him.

There was a window straight ahead. It showed the front of the house. The sun hung there, shining down with everything it had.

He leaned against the window sill and looked down. The roof yawned out around the window and he couldn't see the front drive where he'd left his Mercedes.

It better still be there or I'm screwed.

He turned away from the window and saw the somewhat familiar hallway running the length of the place. His room was nearly halfway down, near the middle. He started walking.

You got to start thinking about the future, Jefferson, he told himself. *How's all this going to look? House full of dead sexual deviants? Not good, buddy. You got to start thinking about how you're going to get ahead of this thing.*

He nodded to himself.

Gotta escape those headlines: Prominent local attorney only survivor of orgy gone awry. *That cannot happen. It would ruin you.*

He nodded again.

You didn't know what you were getting yourself into. You didn't know what kind of people these were. You were just invited by a colleague from the firm.

He nodded more vigorously.

Richie's already got a bit of a record, now doesn't he?

"Yes," Jefferson said. "He does."

You have to start thinking about the future, Jefferson. Your *future. Get ahead of this thing.*

He stood in front of his room. He didn't recall getting there. One minute he was staring out the huge bay window at the foot of the stairs, the next he was nodding to himself, smiling and staring at his closed door.

He sucked in a mouthful of air then blew it out.

"OK," he said and opened the door.

The room was black. The curtains were drawn back and the only light came from behind and around him. He stood there waiting for whatever terribleness inside to come rushing out. When nothing happened, he stepped inside.

The door began to slowly swing shut behind him. Jefferson stopped and caught it, knowing the room would be completely in darkness if the door closed. He squinted off into the murk for something to prop the door open with. There was no doorstop apparent.

He found nothing within arm's reach. He decided he'd have to open the door as wide as it would go, then streak across the dark room to the windows and throw back the curtains to light the room with sunlight.

He squinted out into the darkness and couldn't make much out in the dim room. He knew it was a straight shot to the window and didn't think he saw any obstructions. So long as he kept a straight line he'd be fine, he decided.

He pushed the door back until it moved no further. Then he took a quick breath and let it go, at the same time pushing himself forward at a sprint. Into the blackness he ran, going completely on a trust that he knew the general layout of the room, not able to see his feet pounding the carpet before him.

His foot caught on something and he pitched forward. He threw his hands out before himself to break his fall. They smacked into the glass of the window, which through the curtain he felt break outward. Sharp, stabbing pain erupted near both of his armpits as well as his chest.

He was carried forward by his motion after the trip and shattered the room's window. He pulled the curtain rod out of the wall when he bounced off the window sill and fell to the floor. Harsh light flooded into the room, which Jefferson caught momentarily before the curtains fell across him, blocking it all out.

For a frightening second, he was caught, wrapped up with seemingly no escape from the curtains. They were thick, lavishly soft, but caught easily, entangling him. He screamed with panic and rage and eventually ripped his way out, abrading the corners of his fists with something akin to rug burn in the process.

He sat, his head, shoulders and arms free of the curtains, panting in the sunlight, covered in sweat and bleeding.

Jefferson took stock of his injuries. The cuts under his arms and chest were mostly superficial but bleeding profusely just the same. Under his left armpit was a deep gash where little strings of fat, like rancid curds of boursin cheese, hung exposed to the outside world for the first time. He thought of maggots and dark, damp places and felt sick.

"Jesus," he said.

Then he remembered how that wound had come about: he'd tripped over something in the dark.

He turned his head and saw her.

Caerulean. His ponygirl.

Her eyes were open. Her face expressionless. She was very pale. Her blond hair smeared with dark, dried blood. He then saw the odd shape of the crown of her head. It was pushed in a bit. He'd accidentally backed into a pickup with a hitch one time and gotten a fender dent that looked similar. Something trivial. A hassle, sure, but easy to fix.

"Caerulean," he said.

She did not stir.

"Get up," he said, finding his voice grave, commanding. "I said get your ass up."

He struggled to free himself from the curtains, infuriating him more.

I'll make her listen.

"Obey me. I own you."

He threw the curtains onto the bed. He stomped over to the naked woman, his ponygirl. He toed her, hard, on her left clavicle. He felt it crunch against his toes.

"Get your ass up!" he screamed. "We got trouble."

She's dead.

He stood there and the rage flooded away from him. Ebbed away like a receding tidal wave.

Did you kill her?

He didn't know how to answer himself. He couldn't remember. He didn't think so.

I hope to God I didn't.

There was a pause. Jefferson thought he could hear the other him, the one in control, the one that never lost his cool, run through the gamut of possibilities.

She was beautiful, stunning even in death. She was thin, well-defined, imposing in her passivity.

Roll her over.

He did as he was told. The fractured bone in her shoulder moved disjointedly as he scooped his hands under her to move her. She lay on her side, going along with Jefferson's motion and gravity.

Her head was definitely crushed. A bit more than a simple fender bender. The indentation was about the size of a fist. Her blond hair did a good job of covering up the residual fractures but the spot of impact was too changed to disguise.

You're more of a choke and bite kind of fellow.

Jefferson nodded.

See there? Both buttcheeks? There's your bite marks.

Jefferson knelt and saw.

Yep. Those're probably me.

Of course, they're you. See there?

Where?

Right there. Side of her neck.

Jefferson moved Caerulean's head a bit and saw. There

were dark purple bruises wrapping around her neck. He felt his stomach drop.

No.

Yep. I think you did. Those're a bit more than a little rough play, Jefferson. You got to be more careful. You got careless. Sloppy.

"No," Jefferson said. His voice sounded high, whiney, pleading.

But her head . . .

Yeah, her head is definitely smashed in but do we know for certain that's what did it? The bruising on the neck indicates—

I know what it indicates.

Then stop being such a baby and help me help you get out of this thing. We got to get ahead of it, Jefferson. I hate to tell you this but this is serious.

I know. I know.

OK then.

He rose to his feet and went back to the window. The sun and blue sky mocked him, laughing down with carefree beauty. The forged innocence, the faux simplicity. It made Jefferson ill with hatred. Knowing the sun burned with an uncontrollable rage, flinging off its venomous spit into the cool, dark emptiness. Knowing the sky, cloudless now, was but a front, a tableau for disastrous storms, throwing lightning and tornadoes around like confetti.

"Liar," he said, feeling his mouth fill up with spit.

"Liar, liar," each iteration of the word rising in volume and heat. "Liar!"

His chest heaved and something seemed to flutter in there, beating against his ribs and sternum. He spasmed and coughed. A mist of red burst from within. He saw it twinkle for a split-second in the sunshine before dissipating into unseeable particles, little bits of himself that were no longer his property. Little bits of himself he'd never have back.

Easy, tiger. Calm down. We have to think clearly. Get ahead of

67

this thing.

He set his hands down onto the windowless sill. Shards of glass tinkled under his palms, some biting in and making more cuts. His body felt like cuts and bruises from head to toe. He kept his hands there. Feeling the pinch of pain stab his consciousness back into some sense of rationality.

Shouting at the universe for existing is a little out of our purview at the current moment, Jefferson.

He nodded.

I know. Sorry. I'm here now.

Good. Let's work this out.

The teeth marks'll prove that you hurt her.

She liked it.

Maybe, but that's beside the point. You hurt her. An all vanilla police force and justice system will hold that against you.

SSC though. SSC.

Safe, Sane and Consensual. I know you know but they won't. This could very easily end up being another "Sex Party Turns Deadly" thing. We don't want that.

OK. So what? I can't just remove the bite marks from her ass. I drew blood.

I know you did. Dental records would be a match. Hours would be spent on that fact alone, more than likely, with the prosecutors making you out to be a sexual fiend. Jury tainting is nearly impossible to whitewash, you know that.

Jefferson nodded.

So, we need to flip this thing.

Get ahead of it.

Exactly. Say, you have your fancies, right? Everybody does.

He nodded.

So, you're here, amongst others with similar fancies.

OK.

And somebody, a third party at large, comes breaking into the place. Killing all these sexual deviants. Do I sense some religious fanatics in play? I think I do.

But there is a third party at large. I couldn't have done this.

Jefferson, Jefferson. We need to start accepting our situation. Whether you did kill the bitch or didn't isn't really the point now, is it? We need to get you out of this mess with as little tainting as possible. You're the victim here, right?

But I didn't—

Jefferson. Listen to me, right now. Do you want to spend the rest of your life in prison? Do you really want that lethal injection? Because if you do, I can check out now. I've got other things I can be doing.

Jefferson hesitated. His heart was racing again. It felt like a matchbox car on the track with one wheel missing, tilted and scraping.

OK, he thought finally. *OK. So what's the plan?*

He thought he could hear the corners of the lips of his mental self turn up in a smile.

We got some work to do.

THE PREVIOUS EVENING

"Don't you say anything?"

The eyes registered nothing.

"I asked you a goddamn question."

He wanted to believe he saw the left corner of her upper lip twitch but he couldn't bring himself to.

"Answer me."

He reached out and took her by the throat. The hands that had hung limply at her sides shot up involuntarily to his wrapped around her windpipe.

"Uh huh," he said, smiling. "Thought so. Knew I'd get a reaction out of your somehow, some way."

She let the arms drop back to her side. The placid face took on a labored placid look. She was having to work to appear so deadfish.

Good. It starts.

He wrenched her arm, an Indian burn to an arm, a ratchet of wheeze-inducing pain for a throat.

"I asked you a goddamn question, bitch."

He reached out with his left hand and patted her left cheek, still holding her with his right.

"Don't you ever speak? Don't you have anything to say?"

70

He switched to poking her with his left index finger, what his father always called "the pointer finger."

"Like, 'yes, daddy,' or 'whatever you say, daddy,' or 'please, don't kill me, daddy'?"

He was in it now. Jefferson was there. He'd found that spot, that high you always go running after the white rabbit for. Somewhere in Wonderland it always waits.

"Oh, don't you worry, darling," he said, pulling her face to his until their noses were touching. "I'm not going to kill you. Yet."

He planted a kiss on her dry lips.

"Oh no, baby," he said. "Not yet. We've still got a bit more fun to have, don't we?"

He was behind her, thrusting with all the violence he could find. He reached forward, never slowing, and grabbed a handful of her hair and twisted it in his hand. He pulled back until he could nearly look into her face.

"*You got anything to say now, ponygirl?*" he screamed.

Her eyes were lined with tears. One spilled out as he pumped.

He laughed. He felt it growing inside him until he couldn't stop, could barely breathe, but he wasn't finished with her. He hadn't gotten there again. He had to get there again. She had things to say. She needed to beg for his forgiveness. She needed to plead for mercy.

He let go of her hair, several strands remaining between his fingers, and balled his hand into a fist. Her head slowly bent forward but he caught it with a quick punch before it was out of reach. He heard her grunt in pain.

"That's right."

He reached forward and grabbed another handful of her hair.

"Say it."

He jerked her head back on her neck and spat down into her face.

"Say it! Say it! Say it!" he screamed, nearly there.

"Please," she whimpered. "Stop."

He came.

It rushed from him, a torrent of everything he had filling her and spilling out onto the carpet around them.

He let go of her hair to grab her hips for support. He was still inside, slowing but still moving in and out, getting the last little bit of that brutal ecstasy.

He came to a sputtering stop, pulled out and shoved her by her ass cheeks forward. Caerulean crumpled onto the carpet, sobbing.

There, he thought. *There it is.*

"That's right," he said, gasping. "I knew you'd come around."

He grabbed a handful of the down comforter and cleaned himself up.

"Got anything you'd like to say?" he asked. "Before we go again?"

Her body was shaking. She had her face buried in the crook of her right arm. He could see the whole span of her undercarriage from where he stood. Saw little globs of himself dripping out of her, pooling like cooling lava on the floor.

"Please," her voice was muffled with her face covered. "Please."

Her shaking intensified. The crying noises changed.

"Look at me," he commanded. "Now."

The shaking began to lap, take on a rhythm.

She's laughing, he realized.

"Hey!" he shouted.

She rolled over onto her back. Her face was lit up by her tear-covered smile. Snot, bright green with bits of bright red running like an undercurrent within a larger river ran from her nose and covered her mouth. Her white teeth gleamed under the room's overhead lighting.

She rocked back and forth on her sides, laughing.

Jefferson stood stunned, staring down at his ponygirl, the slave he'd bid on and purchased only a few hours before.

"What are you laughing at?"

Her hands went to her stomach, she was laughing so hard.

"Stop it."

"They'll never let you go," she laughed.

"Stop laughing," he whispered. "Stop it."

"You'll never," she laughed, gasping for breath, "get out of this alive."

"Stop it, stop it!" he yelled.

"Kill," she laughed, "me. Kill me. Kill me."

Jefferson shot away from the bed, his flaccid penis swaying with each step, and straddled her stomach. He hit her in the face with an open hand.

"Stop laughing at me."

Her eyes spilled more tears. More snot and blood ran from her nostrils. She kept right on laughing.

"Why are you laughing at me?"

He hit her again.

"You'll never get out—"

He hit her again.

"—of this alive."

Her voice broke and her laughing doubled.

Bitch is crazy.

"Poor little boy," she laughed.

Jefferson scrambled to his feet and retrieved the empty eighteen-year bourbon bottle. He was back over her before he realized what he was doing.

"Do it," she wheezed.

He brought the bottle down with everything he had left in him.

NOW

He had the curtains with both of his hands. He laid them out on the carpet beside the body, his dead ponygirl. He then dropped to his knees and slid his hands under her cold, rigid body and rolled her over onto them.

Good, good. One more half turn then you can wrap her up them.

He tucked the curtains under her, doing his best not to acknowledge the paternal feeling it stirred in him, then rolled her over, a strange human burrito. Only a few wisps of her blond hair hung loosely from the top and each of her big toes from the bottom.

Good. The fire won't miss her this way. She's the worst of the evidence against you. Get the matches from the desk, by the ashtray.

He got back to his feet and stepped over to the desk. He stared down at the ashtray, the half-smoked cigar there, the unwrapped others beside it. The little bag of coke residue had also somehow found its way there.

Go ahead. You've earned one.

Jefferson scooped up the little baggie and desperately ran his tongue through it. Sharp bitterness filled his mouth. His cracked lips sang the notes of pain.

But there wasn't enough there. He let the baggie drop back

dumbly onto the desktop.

Really?

Shame washed over him.

Really, Jefferson? I'm trying to help you and you're trying to escape off into junkie world? Really?

"I'm sorry," he said.

Yes. Yes, you are. We got work to do, goddamn it. We got to get ahead of this thing. Don't you want to get ahead of this thing?

Jefferson began to whimper.

"Yes," he whispered. "I do."

OK then. Pull yourself together and pick up those damn matches.

THE PREVIOUS EVENING

"Sir?"

Jefferson looked up. He was back in the foyer downstairs. He had no idea how he'd gotten there.

"Are you all right, sir?"

A little shadow man stood just off to his left, his face all disapproving and butlery concern.

"Drink," Jefferson said.

The man shifted and was gone, disappeared somewhere into the shadows only to return some brief moment later with a clinking glass of the eighteen-year, the bourbon.

Jefferson took the glass with both of his shaking hands. He cupped it and carefully brought it to his lips. He squeezed his eyes shut and drained it all in two deep swallows.

"Another."

The shadowman delivered.

"Well, lookie lookie," a woman's voice, somewhere to the right, off in the darkness. "Someone's having one hell of a night, I'd say."

Jefferson moved toward the voice, his feet some foreign craft delivering him without any orders or commands.

76

The darkness surrounded him. He bumped into something, spilled some of his drink onto his stomach. The shocking cold of it caused him to look down. His senses felt dulled but he saw that he was naked. The amber liquid snaked down his stomach, stopped briefly in his navel, then continued down to his raw and sore penis and testicles.

"Come on over here and let's have a little more fun, darling," the woman's voice said.

He felt a frigid and firm hand cup his balls and gently pull him forward. His knees came to rest against the soft pillows of the couch. He felt the warmness of a mouth engulf his penis.

"Oh," he said.

"A little sour with your sweet, dear?" another voice whispered in his ear. "Everybody needs a little hurt, huh?"

Jefferson nodded, his eyes closed, his mouth hanging loosely open.

He felt another set of hands take up his right hand. He felt his fingers warm, teeth drag against his skin.

"Oh," he moaned.

He felt each of his fingers sucked and nibbled on, ending with his pinky. Then sharp fingers dug into his side and neck.

"Don't move, Mr. Wellman," another voice said into his other ear.

"Wha—"

He heard the crunch before searing pain rippled through him. He jerked but was held standing.

"My finger!" he screamed. "Oh God, my finger!"

"Good pain time, Mr. Wellman, is over," the voice whispered. "There are debts to be paid."

The room was too dark. He couldn't make anything out, just blacker darknesses moving in the shadows.

Jefferson felt the blood dripping onto his bare feet then a new warmness around his ring finger.

"No," he begged. "Please."

"Debts and bad pain, Mr. Wellman," the voice whispered.

Then another crunch and everything went black for Jefferson Wellman.

He woke to the sound of steps, booted feet moving through dew slick grass. His eyes opened to his arms dangling and the world moving under him. Legs moved under him but they were not his.

"Wha—"

The legs hesitated then continued.

"—he'll be out again in a minute. No telling exactly how it'll affect—"

His eyes closed without his conscious will. His body felt warm and dull like heavy whipping cream heating in a pan, velvetizing.

A little voice spoke up somewhere in his head.

Hang in there, buddy.

He didn't recognize the voice, though it sounded familiar, and went back into the lazing blackness.

The sound came first then the physical sensation. It was a slapping sound and the first thought that streaked through Jefferson's mind was that he'd passed out fucking. The sound was so similar to thighs meeting buttocks.

Then he felt the sharp, quick smacks on both sides of his face and tried to open his eyes. They wouldn't budge. They felt crusted over.

He tried to open his mouth, tell whoever was slapping him to cut it out, but his mouth felt sewn shut.

"Wakey wakey," a voice, somewhere near, said. "Eggs and bakey."

"Jesus, how much did you give him?" another voice asked, somewhere a little further away.

78

"Enough," the voice nearest answered. "Time to wake up, Mr. Wellman. You don't have to stay awake. I just need you to look and listen for a minute then you can go on back to dreamland."

He wanted to shout that he hadn't been having any dreams. That he didn't know dreams could be found in that engulfing yet comforting blackness. But his mouth wasn't working.

"Didn't factor in all that whiskey, did ya?" the far-away voice asked.

"Shut up."

Jefferson heard movement then a freezing stream of some cold liquid covered his face, filling his nostrils, his open mouth and eye sockets. It went on and on until Jefferson was sure he was going to drown then, suddenly, it stopped.

He was able to flutter his eyes open though they stung and felt like they'd had at least the top two layers removed.

"There's a nice little drinky drink for ya," the voice said.

An impressionistic blur of a person loomed above Jefferson. His eyes wouldn't focus.

"Really like the eighteen-year, don't ya?"

The scent of it then registered in his mind and he knew why his eyes stung.

"OK, now that we're awake we got some things to go over," the shape said.

Another hazy person stepped into view over the right shoulder of the talking shape.

"Thanks to the miracle of modern medicine you probably won't recall this conversation."

"Not exactly."

"Right, not exactly. The specifics of it will elude you. The content, hopefully for you and for us, will remain though."

"Especially for you."

"Right. Now, you're going to go back to sleepy sleep here

79

in a few. In a few hours that bastard, the hot, hot sun, will wake you and bring you back to life."

"Your new life."

"Yes. You'll wake up, see that along with your clothes, you're missing a few other things."

"A few things more near and dear to you."

"Dear, yes. You'll eventually find the path and follow it along to the house where you'll see our handiwork."

"Our meaning us *and* you."

"Handiwork, God, I just said handiwork."

The shapes turned toward each other and laughed.

"Anyway, you'll find the house, the contents of said house and have a decision to make. You'll struggle, you all always do, but in the end you'll make this decision."

"Burn the fucker down."

"Right, bright flames in midday keeps the investigators and prying eyes at bay."

"You're a poet, don't ya know it?"

Jefferson felt the lids of his eyes beginning to slip closed.

"No, no, no, you don't," the voice nearest said. "Not just yet."

A fresh splash of the ice cold bourbon slapped down onto his face.

He gasped and opened his eyes wide.

"Now, once the place is good and cooking—"

"Hot, hot, hot."

"You'll come back here. Right back here where you'll wake up feeling like a ten ton pile of shit in a few hours from this moment."

"The shittiest of shits."

"OK? You got that, Mr. Wellman?"

"Mr. Jefferson Wellman, Esquire."

"You got that, Mr. Jefferson Allen Wellman, Esquire?"

Jefferson felt hands slip under his head, raising it then

rocking it forward in a nodding motion.

"Good."

"Good."

"Now, sleep tight."

"Don't let the bedbugs bite."

The shape nearest shot toward him and Jefferson was thrown back into the blackness.

NOW

We do know the way out of here, yes?

Jefferson nodded, staring at the flame dancing on the end of the match.

Then light 'er up.

Jefferson let the match drop down into the little trashcan, which he'd filled with shredded Post-it notes.

The match fizzled, smoked then went out.

Well, that was anticlimactic. Guess you better give it another go.

Jefferson struck up another match. He knelt and carefully set this one down onto the little scraps of paper. They took and soon the trash can was spitting flames.

Dump it on her.

Jefferson picked up the trash can, using the thick down comforter as a makeshift oven mitt, then upturned its flaming contents onto the human burrito in the middle of the floor. He had to step quickly away to avoid burning his bare feet.

He watched the fire slowly catch and spread across the room with an empty mind. The sudden quietness was comforting as were the dancing shoots of yellow and red and growing tendrils of black-gray smoke. He had the sudden urge to sit down and let go, just let the fire take him. It felt, inex-

82

plicably, like the right thing to do.

OK.

Jefferson shook his head.

OK, now. Time to get moving.

Jefferson pulled the chair out from under the desk and sat down.

Jefferson. What are you doing?

"She said they'd never let me leave alive. What did she mean?"

She was a crazy person. Some stupid, shit-talking bitch.

"She begged me to kill her."

Easy now. We don't know what kind of mental instabilities that . . . that woman had. There's no telling what was going on in her pretty little head. Probably a cluster of maggots eating away what little peabrain she had. What does she matter now, anyway?

He didn't know how to answer himself.

I know how hard these last couple of crazy hours have been. Crazy stuff, this. But what doesn't kill you only makes you stronger, right? Time to get up, get out and get moving on. The room's gonna be really blazing here in a few and it's going to spread much quicker than it took. That's usually the way with fires. I need you to stand up on those cut up feet of yours and get to padding across the room, on through the door, down the hallway, down the stairs and, finally, out the door.

Jefferson didn't reply.

The keys to the car should be on the desk here.

Jefferson turned to scan the contents of the desktop. The keys weren't there.

Well, that does pose an interesting issue but it doesn't negate the fact that this room is on fire and you need to get the hell out, Jefferson.

Jefferson felt the first rush of heat press against him as the bed caught fire. Sweat beaded across his nearly naked body. He pushed himself up from the chair and had to squint against the intense heat. It seemed to suck all the moisture from his eyeballs.

Good. There you go. Come on, buddy, get moving.

Jefferson slid in between the raging cylinder of fire containing his deceased ponygirl, Caerulean, and the smoking wall. He took long, stretching steps, feeling the heat radiate across the bottom of his testicles, the insides of his thighs.

He twisted the knob and opened the door and turned. The flames from the bed had spread to the ceiling like some sort of melting in reverse. The carpet had all but disintegrated. He couldn't make out any of her specifics with the fire lapping but he could see she was still there, burning.

He turned and let the door slowly swing along its axis to close behind him.

The hall was empty. He half-expected the murderous third party to be standing there, waiting. He strode down the hall with the same sure-footed steps and entered the stairwell. He quickly found his way down in the dark, no hesitancy now that it was over.

He opened the first floor door and made his way into the long hall leading to the foyer and the front door.

He heard a muted crash from somewhere far above.

You're doing great, buddy.

Jefferson didn't reply. The hall floor was very cold, a sharp contrast to the room he'd just left. His feet felt confused, having expanded and contracted and expanded and contracted. There were blisters to go with the cuts now. He stepped down with a force that wasn't necessary with each step. He slapped his feet down, willing himself to not show the faintest hint of discomfort. He'd earned the pain. He was deserving of it. Punishment, self-inflicted. Self-flagellation.

He made it to the front door and twisted the knob. It wouldn't turn.

It's locked. Slow down, breathe. Unlock the door first.

He moved his hands up to the deadbolt and found it unlocked.

Try the knob itself.

The little twist lock on the doorknob was unlocked as well.

That's strange.

"Indeed."

He tried forcing the door open with his shoulder but it wouldn't budge. It was a solidly built, very expensive front door.

The back. The way you came in.

Jefferson turned away from the door but stopped short.

What're you doing?

"I have this feeling that the car isn't there anymore."

What? Why wouldn't it be there?

"Why would the door be locked from the outside?"

Jefferson stepped back to the door and looked through the peephole. He could see the entire front of the house and there wasn't a car in sight.

He stepped back from the door, his mind spinning.

Well, OK then. So, let's get ahead of this thing. Your car's gone, somebody obviously stole it. We can use that, yes. OK. You woke up to the place burning, ran outside and your car was gone. Third party murders the people in the house, including the poor, insane girl you were bedding in completely consensual agreement, then steals your car for their getaway.

Jefferson walked through the foyer into the living room with the two couches of dead people.

The curtain he'd thrown back was still open. The room was motionless, heavy with darkness. He couldn't stop himself, he went back to the couches. He wanted to make sure the bodies were there, that they were real, that this entire fucked up morning was real.

They were and it was.

He didn't stare long, he heard another muted crash, this one just a little louder than the other, then there was a tremendous smashing sound from just outside the French doors.

Move, Jefferson.

He swung one of the doors open and stepped out onto the deck. From two stories above him a window had burst outward, smashed onto a patio table, crushing it. The charred and flaming remains smoked up into the clear blue sky.

Move.

Jefferson stepped down onto the deck stairs and didn't look back until he was halfway across the backyard, moving toward the path into the woods. Then he turned back and looked at the mansion. It looked like it was wearing a clown's red wig. Long, flailing flames splashed up toward the sky, shrank back toward the house then leapt back up again. Smoke billowed from all of the third floor windows, which must've all blown out from the intense heat and pressure.

"Jesus," Jefferson whispered.

"Don't be gettin' all religious on me now," a voice from behind him said.

Jefferson swung around so quickly he lost his balance and toppled over.

"Easy there, tiger," the man said.

He stood, leaning against a hackberry elm. The leaves above his head seemed to be burning right along with the mansion not a hundred yards away, they were so violently red.

"Come on, now," the man said. "Up, up, up. We got to get moving. The others are waitin'."

"Third p-p-pa—" Jefferson stammered.

"What?"

"Third party," he was finally able to spit out.

"Third party, huh? Always the consummate attorney,

aren't we, Mr. Wellman," the man said, pushing himself off the tree. "Well, there isn't gonna be any third parties here. You're one of us now, that's that."

"What are you talking about?"

"Debts and bad pain, Mr. Wellman," he said. He stepped onto the path and reached his hand down to Jefferson.

"What?"

Jefferson made to grab the man's hand but stopped short of grabbing it when he noticed this man, too, was missing the ring and pinky fingers of his right hand.

"Yes, yes," the man said, taking another half step to reach his hand down closer to Jefferson. "Welcome to the club."

The man's hand clasped onto Jefferson's and he was pulled back to his feet.

"Let's go. The local yokels'll be here 'fore too long."

The man released Jefferson's hand, turned and started down the path into the woods.

What do I do? he asked himself.

I . . . I don't know.

Jefferson turned, took one last look at the burning house, then followed the man down the path, careful not to get too close.

"Who are you?" he called ahead.

The man didn't stop, slow or give any indication he'd heard the question.

"I said, 'Who are you?'" Jefferson called again.

The man kept right on walking, long steady strides that never seemed to alter or slow.

Jefferson watched the man's shoulders as they continued on under the gold, brown and red leaves. They were held erect, solid. They seemed to move separately from the rest of him.

What is happening?

I don't know. I really don't know.

What should I do? Should I run? Do you think he'd catch me, kill me?

I don't think so. I think you should stay with him. See who or what is waiting at the end of this path. Lord, you can't go back to the house at this point.

The lone wail of a distant siren trickled through the trees overhead.

Hang tight, buddy.

The siren sounds faded as they continued. Jefferson hadn't realized how far he'd walked that morning until now. He must have been at least two and a half miles from the house.

"Where are we going?" he shouted at the man ahead.

The man didn't answer. Jefferson didn't expect him to but he found the silence too ominous not to break.

"Who are you? Where are we going? What's all this about debts and bad pain?"

The man disappeared as the path turned and dropped down, back into the valley in which he'd awoken earlier that morning.

"I've got money, if this is what this is about," Jefferson called.

He hesitated, slowing with the man no longer in sight.

"I said, 'I've got money,'" Jefferson called.

He slowly continued up the path to the slope, shooting wary glances to his left and right and over his shoulder. The man was nowhere in sight.

"Jesus," Jefferson whispered.

"Enough with the religiosity, Wellman," the man said. "We're a little beyond that now, don't you think?"

He was leaning against another hackberry, this one shining golden in the afternoon sunlight.

Jefferson jumped back and nearly tripped again.

"Listen, Wellman," the man said, his eyes burning into Jefferson's. "We've got to get a few things straight. There is no you anymore. Just like there is no me. You and I are now a part of we. We, get it? We've got quite a lot to accomplish this afternoon and if you don't start picking up the pace, you're going to force me to speed you up. And you don't want me to speed you up, do you? Wouldn't you rather just carry your own weight?"

There was a maliciousness in those eyes, not obscured by their brightness. The man would've been handsome if not for those eyes, thick clean-shaven jowls, pouty lips, a full head of hair slicked off to the right and in perfect order. He was tall, taller than Jefferson, and very well built.

Go with it, Jefferson.

Jefferson nodded his head.

"Lead the way," he said to the man.

The man's face lit up with his smile. It was such an easy thing, that smile; it almost covered up for those eyes.

At the bottom of the valley, in the exact place where Jefferson had come to earlier that morning, somebody was waiting. Jefferson saw her, the body was slender and curved, from some distance and couldn't place her. As he descended, a few steps behind the man, he saw that the woman wore a hat.

Coming into the little clearing, Jefferson saw her and placed her: the woman from the room of monitors. She smiled up at him as he approached.

"Afternoon, Mr. Wellman," she said.

"Who are you?"

"Thanks for retrieving Mr. Wellman, Tommy," she said, turning to the other man.

He nodded his acknowledgement and walked around her. He stopped just behind and to the left of her and turned those eyes back on Jefferson.

"What in the hell do you think you're doing?" Jefferson said, feeling himself on the cusp of losing control of his tone and volume.

Easy, buddy.

The woman smiled placidly across the five feet to where Jefferson stood, heart racing and panting. Jefferson saw it for what it was: the smile you give an ignorant, annoying child.

"*Just who the fuck do you think you are, lady?*" Jefferson screamed.

He felt cords in his neck rise, pull tight then twitch under the strain of his anger. His hands balled into fists. Feeling the gaps in his fists pushed his anger further.

"What have you done to me?"

The woman took a sure, steady-footed step toward Jefferson.

The man behind her moved with her but his gaze shifted momentarily to the woman, unease crossing his face.

"Mr. Wellman, I gave you exactly what you wanted," she said. "What you paid for."

"I didn't agree to this!" Jefferson shouted, lifting both hands before him and releasing the fists to show the gaps where fingers used to be.

The woman's gaze did not leave Jefferson's face.

"I didn't agree to any of that . . ." Jefferson faltered, looking for the words.

Murder. Torture. Arson. Destruction of evidence. Fleeing the scene.

The words, terms and actions, floated in his mind and he knew, through years of careful, legal practice, not to utter them aloud. Not to give his opposition any advantage he could help.

Instead of finishing his sentence, Jefferson half turned and waved his right arm back in the direction of the house, or what was left of it.

She was on him as he turned his head back.

Her fingers dug into his throat. One of her legs wrapped around his, right behind the bend of his knees. He crumbled onto his knees, hands clutching at the fingers around his windpipe. He couldn't pry them loose. They were miraculously strong for such a relatively small woman.

The woman's face loomed before his, growing as she inched closer.

"Listen to me, Mr. Wellman," she said, face twitching slightly with the effort but smile still in place. "A lot of work has gone into you. You now no longer exist to the world at large. You died in an unfortunate fire in the hills of eastern Kentucky."

Jefferson's vision began to condense. Floaters filled his vision, little streaking shooting stars in the space between this woman's face and his own.

Her eyes burned with a savagery unparalleled by anything he'd ever experienced, even by the man Jefferson knew was somewhere close behind her.

"You are a cog now, Mr. Wellman," she whispered, her lips curling away from her gritted teeth, the smile widening. "You will serve your function."

Jefferson could feel the blackness washing over him. He was going to lose consciousness, even the floaters beginning to slow.

"Debts and bad pain are your existence now."

Everything faded.

There was lots of shuffling. Pinches in his arms. People talking. Noises he couldn't recognize.

Jefferson tried to open his eyes but couldn't, tried to move any of himself but couldn't.

His thoughts were intangible clumps of sand. Every time he tried to reach down to pick one up, they dissolved before he could even lift them off the ground.

He felt his body sway, limp despite his best efforts, and move under the pressure of gravity, of forces beyond his control.

Hands moved him where they directed.

Helpless.

The lone thought pulsated in his leadened mind like a collapsing neutron star, an interstellar lighthouse spinning and shining, shining and spinning. A guiding light for nothing but emptiness, illuminating nothing but emptiness.

Jefferson wasn't fully aware of his slowly burgeoning consciousness for some time. His head ached dully, felt full of cotton, as did his mouth. He rubbed the palms of his hands on the temples of his head and gently rocked back and forth on his back to distract himself from the pain.

God, oh God. Oh God. No, no, no, no. No. No.

A mantra of unintelligible sounds to help ease the discomfort.

A gentle breeze ruffled his hair down onto his forehead. Jefferson opened his eyes.

He was surrounded by sky. All-encompassing, deep blue-black sky. Clouds somewhere off beyond his naked and bandaged feet. Trickles of stars' diamond twinkling to his right and left.

Jefferson made to sit up and his body, at first, rejected the sudden push to motion. It hurt all over, felt foreign and leaden. He tried again and again until he was able to slowly rock over onto his side and use his trembling arms to push himself up into a hunched over, but erect, sitting position.

His body lurched with a motion separate from his weakness. He looked around himself and saw that he was on a boat. He was surrounded not only by sky but a body of water so vast no shore was in sight.

An expansive quietness also hung around him. He listened for noise, any sort of sound, and only heard the rapidly increasing pulse of the blood in his aching head.

His hands moved slowly, warily up his stubbled cheeks to his ears. They were covered, as was his forehead. A few strands of hair had managed to escape the wrapping and hung loosely.

He swept his remaining fingers over the covering but in his rising panic found no opening. He felt his chest heaving but was unable to hear his own breathing.

He raked his fingers under the wrapping, feeling his nails cut into his forehead, until he was able to find purchase then began to push and pull himself free. Blood, hot against the coolness of the air around him, snaked down his forehead and began to build, dam-like, above and inside his eyebrows.

He ripped the head covering off and held it before his eyes. It was a soiled bandaged. Blood, much older, darker in color than the bright blood he knew came from his frantic removal of the wrapping, coated the inside of the bandages as did patches of his hair and flakes of his skin.

"What?" he knew he'd told his mouth to say, but he heard nothing.

He let the bandage drop to his lap. He moved his hands to the places where his ears should've been. He found only raw places. Places where no semblance of his ears remained. Places where, though he felt no pain, he felt no skin either.

He knew he was screaming but, still, Jefferson could hear nothing.

When he woke next, the sun was hanging hot and heavy above him. He blinked behind the shade of his hand and tried to shake himself awake. He felt completely drained of all energy. He felt a shell of himself. Incomplete.

He sat up and felt the motion of the water jostling underneath him. His hands sought his ears and found them covered once again.

His eyes shot open a little wider and he felt a surge of adrenaline rush through him.

How long have I been out?

He looked up at the sun then at the boat around him. He forced himself to rise, legs spread wide to cope with the motion of the raft and his unsteadiness. His stomach lurched and he was unsure if it was only nausea. He couldn't recall the last time he'd eaten.

From the higher perspective of standing, he reaffirmed that he was definitely on a boat. A yacht and an expansive one at that. He was on the topmost portion of the thing, left to crisp in the sun with his ruined hands and ears.

Dull, hot anger filled him again.

I'll kill that bitch.

You're lucky to be alive.

His mouth dropped open.

What?

You're lucky to be alive. Obviously, they went to a lot of trouble not to kill you. There's no telling how many chances they've had. They could've locked you in that house. They could've just shot and killed you in the woods, left you for the police. They could've rolled you off this to drown out here in the middle of nowhere.

Jefferson blinked and closed his mouth.

They've kept you alive for something. There's definitely a reason you're not dead. At least not yet.

Jefferson stood there, swaying gently with the boat, looking out over the sprawling deck below. There were several people lying out, men and women, mostly undressed, some completely nude, on bright white chairs. Servants waited on them and scurried about with serving platters of food and drinks.

What is this?

94

I don't know.

Jefferson sat down, turned and hung over the edge of the platform. His feet dangled under him, bandaged and searching for purchase. He slid himself down further until hanging on by the insides of his tremulous arms. Just when he thought he could hold on no longer his feet found something to hold his weight.

He eased himself onto a metal railing then onto a walkway leading to a set of descending stairs. He leaned against the railing, feeling dizzy with the effort and his weakness, until catching his breath.

He was standing naked, except for the bandages around his head and feet, on the largest yacht he'd ever seen. He had no clue where he was or who'd taken him captive. The absurdity of it came to him then.

Who are these people? What do they want with me? What do I do?

There was no answer from within.

He walked to the edge of the stairs and looked down at the deck below. No one so much as glanced in his direction.

Surely, they know I'm here. They can't all be in on it, can they?

Using the railing, he made his way down the stairs.

He stepped onto the deck and felt the heat radiate up through the wrappings on the soles of his feet. The sun was high in the sky and hammering down onto the boat. Sweat ran in rivulets down his chest and back.

"Help."

He felt his mouth open with his brain's command. He knew he was going through the correct motions of creating sound but still heard nothing. This made him question himself.

No one acknowledged him. The sunbathers bathed, eating or drinking or snoozing. The servants served, bringing drinks, taking away empty glasses and plates.

Jefferson walked to the nearest lounging person, a topless middle-aged woman with enormous fake and well-tanned breasts.

"Help me, please."

The woman did not open her eyes. The sun radiated down onto her browning skin and her face remained impassive.

Jefferson knelt over her, his shadow blocking the sun from her face. The woman's face changed, a look of discomfort washing over her features, her heavily collagened lips pouting, tightly cracked crow's feet appearing at the corners of her eyes. She opened her eyes, took in Jefferson in the briefest of glances then turned over on her side, away from him, and continued her snooze.

Jefferson stared down dumbly at her then stumbled away, toward the next nearest person.

He watched a servant reach down, retrieve an empty glass from a table beside a well-oiled, sleeping man and turn to leave. Jefferson slapped a hand on the man's shoulder before he could stride away.

"Help me. Help me."

The servant stood there, erect, balancing the glass on a tray with his right hand, his left resting at his side. He made no move to turn or acknowledge Jefferson.

"Help me, please. God, please help me."

With one fluid, very quick motion, the servant shot forward, away from Jefferson and out from under his weak grasp. The servant did not turn around but simply walked across the sun-drenched deck to a cabin at the other end.

What is this?

I don't know.

Jefferson tried three more sunbathing people. No one would acknowledge his existence, other than to turn away if he blocked their sun. He stumbled toward the cabin at the end of the dock.

The door was closed but unlocked. Jefferson opened it and stepped into the coolness of air conditioning. The sweat cooled and caused a prickling to run the course of his skin. His testicles ascended and he cupped his penis in his hands.

It was much darker in the cabin, shielded from the overbearing oceanic sun, and it took several moments for his eyes to adjust. Jefferson stood there, holding himself and shivering.

He saw a staircase in the center of the room, descending lower into the bowels of the boat. There were also two halls, each leading off around the stairwell.

The smell of cooked meat and spices filled his nostrils. His stomach churned emptily and drove him forward. The flooring, just a few steps into the door, changed into lush carpeting. His feet sank into it and the urge to lie down and luxuriate in the softness struck him. He banished the thought with another growl of his stomach.

The room was filled with framed art, each appearing to be original oil on canvas as opposed to reproductions. The room was furnished with a large leather couch and two matching armchairs. A bar ran along the wall opposite the couch. A servant was busy filling three highball glasses from a metal shaker. The man didn't so much as look in Jefferson's direction.

Jefferson approached the bar.

"Can I have a drink?"

He knew he had formed the words and had let them leave his mouth, his cracked and torn lips ripped a little more with the motion, but he still heard nothing and the man behind the bar did not respond in any way. The servant continued making the drinks, finished pouring them then dressed them with a little umbrella and a sprig of mint each.

Jefferson leaned onto the bar, the coolness sending his

body convulsing in fresh shivers. He reached out to the servant who, feigning not to notice Jefferson, subtly stepped backward and away from his grasp.

"Enough," Jefferson tried to shout.

He slammed the palms of his hands down onto the polished wood of the bar. He should've heard the slap of his skin but all he felt was the sting of it and the deeper, more troubling ghost pain of the missing fingers.

The servant picked each drink up and, one by one, set them down onto a serving tray and left the cabin, sending a wave of radiating heat and bright sunshine in behind him through the door.

Jefferson leaned across the bar, his chest heaving, ears ringing with nothing but his rapid pulse, and set his right cheek down onto the cool bar surface.

What have I done to deserve this?

Jefferson let himself have a little break. He cried and knocked over the metal shaker the servant had left, empty, on the bartop. When he'd finished crying enough to feel anger again, he pulled himself back to a standing position. He turned to go back toward the center of the room, still unsure whether he'd take the stairs or one of the two surrounding halls, but stopped short, one hand still on the bar.

Might as well have a little drink, he told himself.

He walked the length of the bar and around the corner. The carpet ended, a thick wood covering the floor behind the bar. He walked along the gently rocking fluid—some amber, some clear, some brightly colored—until he found a bottle of Woodford Reserve. He took it down from its place, set it on the bar, and looked around for a whiskey glass.

Under the bar were several different glass types but no whiskey glasses. He turned back to the bar to look in one of the cabinets off to the right of the bottles.

The door to the cabin opened, filling the room with heat and light again. Jefferson made to turn around but stopped himself.

No one is going to acknowledge me. Find the glass. Have a drink.

In the second cabinet he opened, he found a stack of crystal whiskey glasses, not unlike the kind he had at his condo in downtown Lexington. He picked the nearest one up, closed the cabinet door and turned back to make his drink.

The bottle of Woodford Reserve was gone.

What the hell?

Jefferson quickly scanned the room but it was empty. The cabin door had since shut itself and there was no one to be seen.

Not five seconds could've passed. They must be just around the corner.

Jefferson came out from around the bar with as much speed as he could manage without toppling over.

"Hey!" he went through the motions of calling out. "Hey, get back here!"

His feet sank deeply into the carpet, slowing him slightly. He looked first down the hall to the left of the stairwell. He saw nothing but a long hall, longer than he imagined it could've been when he first entered the room, little portholes lining the left wall, door knobs and framed paintings on the right. He looked down into the stairwell but saw nothing but the landing some ten or fifteen feet below. He looked to the right down a mirror image of the hallway to the left.

What the hell?

Tears filled his eyes again. Jefferson wiped them away roughly.

Fuck this. I'm better than this. I will not let this happen. I will not.

Jefferson chose the right hallway.

He slowed as he passed by each closed door. He thought about knocking on them but felt deeply troubled about what he'd see behind the doors. He was, at once, both glad and disarmed by not being able to hear a thing. He didn't want to hear what was happening behind some of these doors but also wanted to be able to hear an attacker coming.

He looked out one of the portholes and saw nothing but sea and sky. No land in sight. He could see the end of the hallway approaching, just another wall turning inward. He had the disconcerting feeling he'd been down this hall already. That he'd been wandering, lost, down a long vaguely familiar hallway for some time. He shook it off and rounded the corner.

Straight ahead the hall to the left of the stairwell met this one. To his right, Jefferson saw another, shorter but much wider hallway. There were no portholes in this hallway. It was lined with wider, more elaborately decorated doors and larger, more expansive paintings.

He stepped into this hallway. The only lighting was from exposed bulbs in ornate fixtures, two to a set, lining each of the thick wooden doors.

There was an unsettling stillness about this hall. He couldn't feel the motion of the ocean under his feet and had nothing to note that the boat was constantly in motion, nothing to note that he was on a boat at all.

He stepped closer to the thickly framed painting nearest him. It was done up in thick blotches of paint, reds and blacks and a little purple. It depicted, roughly, an act of violence. A man, clad only in spattered blood, stood atop a pile of corpses, their mouths agape, eyes unseeing. Some appeared to be screaming and reaching out in agony. The man held his hands out toward the viewer of the painting, an act of supplication or presentation. His penis was half erect and also covered in blood. There were no whites to the man's eyes, just an engulfing blackness unpenetrated by any light or color.

Jefferson moved to the first door, just to the right of the gruesome painting. He saw that it was unlike any door he'd ever encountered. It was intricately and skillfully carved. The door was covered from top to bottom in an immense scene of debauchery, a panoply of horrors. There were hundreds of people killing other people. His eyes moved across the door quickly but he saw that all of the little depictions shared one common trait. They all depicted murder by strangulation.

What is this?

He stepped away from the door and back toward the center of the wide hallway. He turned and went to the door opposite the Choke Room, as his mind dubbed it. This door was also meticulously carved.

I don't want to be here. I don't want to be here.

His eyes widened as they ran over images of people being flayed alive. Hundreds of them, maybe a thousand. Little scenes of personal castration or the removal of skin or fingers or whole appendages. Dozens of sliced wrists and throats. The removal of tongues, noses and, much to Jefferson's horror, ears.

He stepped backward and tripped. He plopped down onto the thick carpeting without so much as a grunt or thump that he could hear. He scooted away from the doors, back the way he'd come, looking down the short but wide hallway, lined by framed paintings, exposed bulbs and disgustingly carved doors.

He counted at least another six doors lining both sides of the hall before it ended in black double doors at its head.

What is this place? Who are these people? What have I done to deserve this?

Jefferson scampered to his feet and backed out of the wide hall.

I'm not going to die here. I'm not going to let these people kill me.

He turned and went back the way he'd come.

Well, if you don't want to die here, on this boat, you better find some food. Some clothes would probably be for the best too.

He stopped and squinted out one of the porthole windows again. He still couldn't make out even the faintest hint of land. Just miles and miles of flat ocean and unending sky.

He made his way down the hall without seeing anyone. Back in the cabin barroom he turned and peered through the window of the door and watched the people lounging about on the deck. They were all carefree, oblivious to his suffering.

How can anyone be so uncaring?

Jefferson turned around and descended the stairs into the bowels of the ship.

He could smell the kitchen long before he found it. Had his ears been working, Jefferson was sure he would've heard the noisiness of a busy cookery from the cabin barroom upstairs. The halls under the ship were not carpeted, nor lined with paintings. They were bare and plain, designed only to serve the servants. Function over any sense of aesthetic.

Doors led off the main hall, to storage rooms, laundry machines, the engines driving the mammoth boat, and the sleeping quarters of the servants. Jefferson did not enter any of these. He went straight for the kitchen, the smell of cooking meat too much of a pull to be denied.

He found the two swinging doors leading into the large kitchen and pushed them open. No one looked up from their tasks. No one gave any notice that a naked man, completely disheveled, wide-eyed, with missing ears and fingers stumbled into what could've passed as a four-star kitchen, had it been back on land and attached to a hotel or restaurant instead of a yacht.

Sitting not ten feet inside the double doors was the serving

102

counter. Plates elaborately decorated with small portions of meat and vegetables sat steaming up toward the massive fans and heat lamps above.

Jefferson changed his impression on the kitchen after seeing the display and whiffing the smells.

Definitely a five-star.

Sitting there, beautifully presented on the plates he knew must've cost a small fortune, were French dishes: baked camembert, cassoulet; Italian dishes: carbonara, Cicero e Trial; Spanish dishes: paella, albondigas; and thickly cut but reasonably sized slabs of filet mignon. Jefferson couldn't help himself. He didn't recall taking the steps to the serving counter or taking up the meat in his bare, dirty hands or ripping into it with an absolute abandon but he knew he must've. The next conscious thought he had came to him some time later. He was looking down at five empty plates on the counter, a trail of sauces and crumbs leading to where he stood leaning on the serving counter, feeling the heat from the lamps above.

His stomach worked busily. He felt the juices congealing on his chin and lips. With the warmness of the food in his belly and from the lamps radiating down onto him, Jefferson felt his eyelids begin to droop. He braced himself on the counter and tried to shake the sleepiness away.

He looked up from his feast at the servants, the cooks, the dishwashers. They didn't so much as bat an eye in his direction. The cooks seemed to be in a frenzy of preparation though.

Probably having to work double now that I've demolished five of their dishes.

Jefferson smiled.

Fuckers. They notice me now.

He started laughing, a faint chuckling that gently shook his shoulders and bobbed his heavy head on his neck. He turned away from the counter, forcing himself to not stuff more food in his mouth, and went out the way he'd come, through the double doors.

The hall outside the kitchen brought goosebumps rippling across his body. Away from the stovetops, ovens, and heating lamps, he felt the coolness of the interior of the boat. It started from the bare flooring under his feet and spread up across the backs of his thighs all the way to the matted hair on his head.

Clothes.

Jefferson went to the first door he came to and eased it open.

He felt so tired. His senses numbed by his full belly. He wished desperately, for he didn't know how many times, that he could hear.

Behind the door was a squat, rectangular room of bunks, stacked two-high up to the short ceiling. No one was in the room. He stepped inside and closed the door behind himself.

There were little closets set off the ends of the bottom two bunks. He pulled open the small sliding closet door and found a little set of shelves, clothes carefully folded and tucked inside each. He riffled through until he found a shirt and pair of slacks that would fit him.

He dressed quickly, shivering under the fluorescents of the room. He didn't find any shoes that would fit. There was a full-length mirror, very cheaply made, which barely reflected his own image back at him, in the corner of the bunkroom.

It was enough to give him a glimpse at his appearance. Jefferson recognized himself. He didn't lie to himself with that old cliché. He knew the person standing before him, looking crazed and horror-struck, was himself. He just didn't think he'd look so utterly different.

How many days has it been since the party? How much weight have I lost? What have they done to me?

Patches of hair covered his scalp. Little burrs where an uncaring clipper or pair of scissors cut around for purposes he knew not what. He gingerly tested the areas with his remaining fingers. Little scabs coated the bald spots, stubbles of hair growing around and through them.

What have they done to me?

Jefferson's stomach lurched.

He recognized the good bone structure, the well-placed eyes and pouty lips. He saw all these features but they were shadows, merely the faintest outline of handsomeness of what couldn't have been but a few days ago.

He stooped lower and moved closer to the mirror which, though technically reflecting back his image, was very poorly made and allowed no great detail to be seen.

Jefferson saw the holes in his skin on each side of his head where his ears used to be. Thick, angry red holes screamed out. He carefully searched them, felt the dried, scaly scabs then the crusted over holes leading inside his head to his eardrums.

If they're even still there.

His gaze shifted back to his face. He looked into his own eyes. They were spiraled with little busted veins. He thought one of his pupils looked quite a bit larger than the other. His eyes, sunk back impossibly far in his skull, looked craven, sleep deprived, thick, sunburned purple bags encasing them.

What have they done to me?

All of the food he'd eaten came rushing up. He sprayed the mirror and was rocked from his feet with his sickness. He dropped onto his hands, his shaky arms barely supporting his weight, and threw up more. His body clenched and convulsed with the force of it. He felt the stolen pants fill with shit and piss.

Oh God, what have they done to me?

He let himself drop to his elbows. He held that position for a few moments, feeling the wetness in both the front and back parts of the pants spread, combine and stale. Then he rolled over onto his back and wept.

Jefferson drifted into an uncomfortable, fitful and accidental slumber. He half-woke several times, sensing movement from both inside and outside the little bunkroom. He was certain at least one and, with all probability, several servants entered and exited the room. He was not touched. He was not moved. Not even acknowledged as far as he could tell.

When he came back from the darkness, he sat up. He smelled himself and fought the urge to retch again. He slowly rose to his feet, the sogginess shifting about in his pants, dried chunks of what looked like the baked camembert flaking off and falling from his servant's shirt.

A wave of dizziness swept over him when he stood fully. He leaned against the closet door until it passed then retrieved another set of the servant's clothing.

Find a shower.

He didn't bother removing the pants or the shirt he'd soiled. He decided to do that after he found a shower and had cleaned himself up.

He left the room and re-entered the cold, bare hallway. He looked to his right and left. He could see the stairway ascending to the cabin's barroom at one end of the hall and the double doors to the kitchen at the other. Somewhere, behind one of the dozens of doors between the two points, had to be the showering facilities.

Nobody wants a dirty servant. There has to be a shower down here somewhere.

He shook at the thought of searching through the rooms above. The thick, horridly carved doors blossomed in his mind like a bloodstained shirt.

He set about opening the doors in the servants' hall. He found many other dorm rooms like the one he'd just left.

106

There's gotta be over fifty servants on this boat.

He tried to recount how many rooms above he'd seen. He estimated at least eight along the hall he'd walked before finding the wide hall with the evil paintings and carved doors.

That's eight on the other side too, then. And at least seven more in that last hallway.

He opened a door and found the laundry room, industrial-sized washing machines busy churning what looked like tablecloths and driers wafting the smell of freshly cleaned linen.

He let that door close on its own and went on to the next.

Bingo.

He stepped inside a room lined with narrow, cramped stalls, above which hung little showerheads. He stripped his shirt off and flung it to the corner to the right of the door, where it would be hidden whenever the door opened. He then set about stepping out of his shit and piss filled pants. As he slid them down his thighs he had to really push and shove, the pants sticking to him with a suction that made his stomach shift uncomfortably. The smell was awful. He took his breaths in quick gulps, holding it for the most part, until he had the pants off and thrown aside.

He opened the nearest shower stall and fiddled with the knobs. A jet of cold water poured down. He turned and turned the knobs but the water would not warm.

No hot water for the servants.

He caught his breath and stepped under the stream. The pressure was intense. The cold water pinged onto his scalp, stinging the little bare spots as well as the holes where his ears used to be.

He squeezed his eyes shut. His breath hissed through clenched teeth.

God it hurts.

He held still until the pain became something he could tolerate. Slowly, steadily he found he could relax. He moved to let the water hit other parts of his body. He moved his nubbed hands, helping the water remove the crust, the dirt, the piss, the shit.

He opened his eyes and scanned the interior of the stall. There on the wall was a little dispenser of two-in-one soap and shampoo. He pumped it and lathered his hands and did his best to clean himself.

Stepping out of the stall, cold water streaming off his naked but cleaner body, Jefferson set about searching the cabinets along the wall for towels. He found them and dried himself. He then retrieved the servants clothes he'd set just outside the stall and dressed. The white shirt and black slacks of a servant. The clothes did not feel right against his skin.

Now what?

Now, we find a way out. We got to get ahead of this thing, Jefferson. We have to get ahead of it.

He nodded to himself. He opened the door and slipped back into the hallway.

They know you're awake. They've obviously seen you. You're not invisible.

What are they waiting on?

I don't know. I guess they're seeing how you react.

Why?

Proving a point? That anybody, even a man of stature like yourself, can be made into nothing. That's my best guess, Jefferson.

That's fucked up.

Yes, it is.

What are we going to do about it?

I'm not sure just yet. We're going to have to play this one by ear.

Jefferson moved down the hallway, back toward the stairs and the cabin above.

Just a few days ago, I had it all.

Stop that, now. This is not the time.

I had status, a great job; privilege. Privilege, goddam it. I had the freedom to do just about anything I wanted to. I could've done anything I wanted. Anything.

Pull yourself together, Jefferson.

His face twitched. The sides of his face jerked up and down and quivered. Tears welled in his eyes but did not spill.

It just goes to show you that you just never know, you know?

You sound like a soccer mom, kid. Shut the hell up and pull yourself together.

Jefferson nodded and screwed up his face then let out a long exhalation.

OK. I'm OK now.

Good.

Jefferson padded up the steps, still barefooted. The barroom in the cabin was empty. He resisted the urge to go pull a bottle, any bottle, from the bar and slink away into some dark corner with it. Just pour vodka or gin or whatever into his mouth until he was somewhere else again.

He opened the door out onto the deck and the sunlight dazzled him. It felt like the sun was hanging just mere inches above the yacht. Sweat prickled up through his pores and started flowing freely down his spine, bringing the coarse shirt sticking against his skin.

He stepped off to the side of the door, seeing the vague shape of someone approaching. He kept his hand over his squinted eyes, wishing they'd adjust faster.

The shape turned out to be a servant who, of course, did not acknowledge Jefferson in any way. The man opened the door, fleeting wisps of the cool air conditioning rushing out to tickle Jefferson's exposed, sweating neck.

His eyes adjusted and he moved across the deck, back in the direction he'd come initially. He passed sleeping, sunbathing men and women. They did not stir. They did not bat an eye.

I'm not so sure I'm not invisible.

You're not.

How can you be so sure?

Look at your feet.

He looked down and saw his shadow looming there, small but visible, before him.

Oh.

Yeah. Pull yourself together.

He came to the foot of the rising stairs leading to the platform on which he'd woke. He started up and made it nearly to the top when a woman appeared at the head of the stairs. She wore a red floral-printed sundress. In the gentle but consistent breeze, the hem of the dress ruffled very high up on her tan, muscular thighs. She wore impossibly high high-heels.

She crested the top of the stairs and started down, all confidence. She didn't use the rail for a second. She shot one foot out over the precipice of nothing then stomped it home on one of the metal stairs with a clang that sent gyrations up the rest of her well-curved body.

Her auburn hair was loose and fluttering with both the motions of her movement and the oceanic breeze. Her face was made up heavily, her lips too red, her eyes too enshadowed with a bruise-like purple. Her eyelashes, which must've been fake—no human eyelashes in Jefferson's opinion could ever reach those lengths naturally—were as dark as the day was bright.

She strode down the middle of the stairs, one commanding, slapping step after another. Jefferson was forced to move out of the woman's way before she barreled directly down on him. He leaned as far over the stair railing as he could and held his breath as she passed by.

A heavy scent of something beginning to rot wafted after her. Jefferson pictured a pile of funeral flowers liquefying together some weeks after the body was lowered. But there was a taste of sweet in the decay. Even rotting flowers held some shred of their former beauty.

Jefferson watched her descend. The dress flicked and fluttered across her ass and Jefferson felt himself shifting in his servant's slacks.

Jesus.

He wondered what she tasted like before he could trace or stop his line of thinking.

He couldn't pull his eyes off the woman. He watched her strut across the deck, past the sunbathers, who sat up and acknowledged her presence with nods of salutation and what looked like hushed whispering in her wake.

When the woman was almost to the cabin door, she turned and looked up at Jefferson. He felt his stomach drop. Everything in him felt like it spontaneously turned to sand and sifted through to the stairs under his feet. He felt his mouth drop open and his gnarled left hand clamp down harder on the railing.

Jefferson watched in astonishment and confusion as the woman lifted both of her hands, the sun reflecting off her heavily lacquered and red painted fingernail extensions, and placed them over both of her ears. She held them there and, despite the distance, Jefferson was sure she smiled up at him.

The woman in red turned and disappeared behind the closing door of the cabin.

What the fuck? What the fuck was that?

Jefferson stood there waiting on an answer.

Eventually, his gaze turned back to the sunbathers and servants on the deck below. Their avoidance of looking in his direction was obvious. Had he had ears, he felt they would be burning with their discussion of him and the woman in red.

The sunburned backs of those in the chairs below seemed to mock him. The white shirted servant's refusal of his existence stung him.

That bitch knows something. She knows what happened to my

ears.

Jefferson started down the stairs, feeling his insides reconstitute themselves, harden.

That bitch might've been the one who took them. She's probably the one who took my fingers.

With each step down, Jefferson felt himself solidify. The weakness of only a few moments ago had fled him completely. He felt like steel. He felt like a blade.

That bitch, he thought. *I'll show her.*

He stalked across the deck, forgetting the servants and the sunbathers, and jerked open the door to the cabin. The coolness struck his face and he had to blink back tears. He bumped into something but refused to slow or be moved from his path.

A servant was sent sprawling onto the floor, a tray of drinks splashing down onto the thick carpeting.

Have to acknowledge me now, fucker.

He smelled her much more strongly in the contained cabin, no wind to carry the scent away. She'd taken the hallway to the left. He followed.

His pulse hatefully hammered in his temples. He knew, if his ears worked, he'd hear his ragged breath raging from his open mouth. He was seething.

I'll kill that bitch. I'll kill that bitch for what she's done to me. What she's taken from me.

Had he been able to hear, Jefferson was sure, his feet would've sounded like sledgehammers dropping in quick succession down the hall. He felt he could rip apart anything put in his way, be it a person, a monster, a steel wall of this boat, it didn't matter.

She'll pay. I'll make her pay.

He rounded the corner at the end of the hall and found himself standing, panting, at the foot of the wide hallway, the weird paintings and thick, carved doors before him.

The lighting of the hall was different. That was the first thing he noticed after coming to the realization he had no idea which room the woman had disappeared into. The smell of decay seemed to come from everywhere, each of the doors, the walls, the paintings even. The little bulbs, which hung two to each door, had been covered. Little plastic bags had been dropped over them, painting the hallway a deep crimson.

Jefferson felt his anger flicker.

What is this?

He cautiously stepped further into the hall.

The eerie lighting cast shadows from the light fixtures out into the center of the hall like the frail, thin arms of the dead. The shadows lined the hall, leading to the great double doors at the end some fifty feet away.

God, I wish I could hear.

He took a half step then another, each step seeming to intensify the smell of rot, of decay, of death.

There was a fluttering of motion to his left just beside the third door on that side of the hall. The little plastic bag over the light fluttered again. Jefferson slowly walked over to it. He kept his eyes switching from the bagged bulb to the door beside it.

The little bag shook atop the light bulb. He looked up at it and then smelled the thick, acrid scent of burning. A little flame, as if waiting for just that moment, erupted from the top of the bulb. It spread quickly, almost like water gurgling up from a fountain to slowly slide back down, the fire covering the entire bulb. A thin, gray stream of smoke crawled upward toward the ceiling.

The smell seemed too strong for one little red plastic bag to be burning. Jefferson turned and scanned the hall and saw the bags on the other lights following suit, erupting into little candles. The lighting of the room radiated from red to a blazing yellow to a near white.

113

With a pulse and a static-like feeling in the air that teased the hair on Jefferson's arms and neck, the lights flashed out and the hallway was washed in darkness.

Instinctively, Jefferson fell to a crouch and pulled himself inward, limiting the portions of his body available to attack.

Oh, God. Oh, God.

He knew, if he could hear, he was whimpering. Or, at least, moaning low from somewhere in his throat. But the only thing he could hear was the frantic rhythm of his pulse in his head. His head felt choked with the pounding of his own blood.

"*Who's there?*" he screamed.

He knew he couldn't hear a response, if one was even given, but couldn't stop the gesture anyway.

"*Who's there, goddamn it?*"

The darkness felt pregnant. Jefferson knew someone was there. He didn't know if it was the woman in red, the man with the murderous eyes, the woman from the room full of monitors or some new monster, some ruthless killer there to dispatch him, piece by piece, to be dumped overboard for the sharks.

Oh, God. Oh, God.

He felt more than saw a stir to his left and dove with everything he had away from it. He felt one of the muscles in his groin pull and pang miserably. Then he struck something solid, the wall or the door probably, and everything became a different kind of black from the hall. The kind of black he'd gotten to know quite well since the night of the party.

Hands—some raking, some coddling, some caressing—slithered across his body. He wasn't sure if they were the same pair. They all felt calloused and malevolent, even the caressing one, especially that one.

Jefferson was still in darkness. This wasn't the kind he'd

114

just emerged from though. His eyes, he felt them flickering with his conscious will to move them, just would not see. He felt something against his face, on his eyelids, blocking out any sight.

He struggled to remove the covering but found he was bound. He struggled in pure panic for some time before giving it up as futile. He felt his body, separate from his intentions, begin to quake. He felt the muscles quiver and then he heard his own muffled whimpering.

I can hear. Holy God, I can hear.

"Where am I?"

There was no answer. Jefferson lay where he was strapped, not fighting against his bonds, just listening.

"Who are you?" he asked the darkness.

Lying completely still he could feel the motion of the ocean somewhere below the keel of the boat.

"Who are you people?"

There was the faintest wisp of a touch on the bottom of his left foot. He wasn't sure if it was a touch or the gentle blowing of the air conditioner until he felt it again, some few seconds later, on the bottom of his right foot.

"Who's there?"

His eyelids fluttered against their bonds. Try as he might, he couldn't see a thing.

His feet moved unconsciously away from the touch. His skin felt like it was crawling right off his body.

"Stop it," Jefferson said, hearing his voice crack and hating himself for it.

A few more moments passed in silence. He wasn't touched again. He didn't say anything. He just lay and listened, trying to quiet his breathing to hear better.

Then he felt the touch again, moving slowly up his left shin bone toward his kneecap. He could hear the hairs on his leg deflect off the object, which he was sure was something metal from the sound it made—something akin to a razor moving against his throat when shaving.

His entire body clenched, from his toes to his anus to his already shut eyes, which were closed against his will.

"Stop this," he said. "Stop this right now."

He put everything he had into sounding commanding, to sounding the way he did in the courtroom, in the meeting room, in his life from days past—which now felt years, many years, buried in the life of another person—but it was to no avail. He could hear his voice for what it was: terrified and pitiful.

Oh God, what have they done to me?

As the touching, still very light against his skin, moved up his shin and topped the mound of his kneecap, he felt light-headed. He felt like he was going to pass out. The touching moved up his thigh, dipped somewhat inward until it came to his penis and testicles then moved around at the very last moment. He felt the touching move up his groin, trace the outline of his left hip bone then proceed up to his navel cavity.

Jefferson was shaking all over. He couldn't stop himself from doing it.

The touching stopped at his bellybutton before suddenly disappearing.

He did his best to listen over his ragged breathing but could hear nothing from the darkness around him.

Then the touching resumed, this time at his right shoulder. It moved slowly down his arm, skimming the crook of it like a straight razor, until it reached his hand. He felt the metallic object, he was almost sure it was a razor or knife, stop on the nub where his pinky finger used to be. He knew it was pointed when it began to slowly build in pressure, puncturing the healing wound slowly, methodically.

"Stop it," Jefferson whispered. "Stop it, right now."

116

The pressure incrementally increased until Jefferson knew he was bleeding all over again. He could feel the pulse in his arms beating the blood toward his hand, to the hole opening up in his pinky stub.

He tried to move away from the pain. He tried to squirm his hand further into the restraint around his wrist but it was too tight. He shook and fought against his bonds but was unable to do much more than shiver.

The metal object suddenly eased. It moved across his hand. He could feel it catching and spreading his blood as it slid to the stump where his ring finger used to be. It circled the wound, slowly shrinking until it was no longer moving around but down. The same piercing pain flooded up Jefferson's arm. He felt that wound reopen and more of his blood flow.

"Drink it," a voice commanded from the darkness. He couldn't tell if it were a man's voice or a woman's, the tenor was somewhere in between.

Jefferson heard the sudden catch of someone's breath, somewhere off to his left. He tried to turn his head toward the sound of scuffling drawing near but the restraints held him still.

"Don't waste a drop," the voice said.

The voice was disconnected from the noises of movement. The voice had receded.

"That's right," the voice said. "Do as I say."

Jefferson felt a wetness different from his bleeding on the outside of his right hand. He felt the distinct texture of a tongue move across his hand. Then he heard sucking sounds and felt the mouth move over the twin holes where his pinky and ring fingers used to be.

"That's enough," the voice said.

It sounded breathier than it had earlier.

"*What is this?*" Jefferson cried.

He felt the mouth move away from his hand, felt a string of saliva pull taut then snap back onto his knuckles.

"Why are you doing this?" he asked.

"Come," the voice demanded.

Jefferson listened to the unmistakable sound of someone crawling across carpet, moving away from him, somewhere toward his feet, toward the voice.

"Good boy," the voice cooed. "Good boy, who's a good boy?"

He heard the sound of patting.

"That's right," the voice said. "You're a good boy."

Jefferson began to cry. He couldn't stop himself. He tried to hold his breath, hoping the lapse in control would pass, but all it did was make him dizzy and gasp.

"Now, do exactly what I tell you," the voice spoke in a register reserved specifically to pet owners and parents.

The touching started again on the left side of his body, near his ankles. It was obviously a different person wielding the knife now. The pressure was tenuous, sometimes making barely any contact with the skin at all, sometimes too much, leaving gashes and scrapes across his leg as it moved slowly, unsteadily upward.

"Good," the voice said. "That's it. Just like that."

The knife nicked against the base of his kneecap and Jefferson knew he was bleeding.

"Oops," the voice said. "Now, you have to be careful. Can you be a careful, good boy?"

The tone of the voice was light, a parent allowing a child to help bake the cookies, and very self-assured. There was no question, despite who held the knife or razor or whatever it was cutting Jefferson's body, who was in charge.

The knife's touch against Jefferson's knee lightened then moved up and over toward his thigh. As it moved closer to his middle, he felt it slow, shake under the unsteady hands. Then it moved unmistakably inward, toward his groin.

"Now, now," the voice gently chided.

The knife wavered not two inches from Jefferson's genitals. He held his breath then let it out and took it back in in quick gulps.

The knife moved so close he felt it tease the hair around his stomach before moving to the center. It stopped at his bellybutton and turned around, headed back south.

The voice did not intercede.

The knife moved, shakily and slowly, back down and stopped at the base of Jefferson's penis, following its length and resting lightly at the tip.

"All right, then," the voice said. "That's enough."

The knife remained where it was.

The voice hardened and grew quieter.

"I said that's enough," it said.

"Please," Jefferson whispered. "Please don't."

The knife lifted then dropped, lifted then dropped, lightly but not lightly enough. Jefferson felt the cuts, superficial but painful, spread about his penis.

There was a quick burst of movement, the sound of clothes moving then the thump of a fist or hand or object meeting with a body. The knife on his penis was gone for a second then he felt it hit the table—or whatever it was he was lying on—between his legs. He felt the blade point jab at his anus and he tried to move away but couldn't.

Jefferson heard the groan of pain then the crying whimpers.

The point of the blade jabbed his rectum with every breath he exhaled.

"Me sorry," a gruff man's voice said from somewhere under Jefferson. "Me sorry, me sorry."

Jefferson heard the sound of movement again then another

thump and more crying from the floor. Then the body of the voice brushed against the table and descended upon the crying good boy.

"No, no!" the good boy screamed. "Me sorry! Stop, please!"

Then there was the sound of fist meeting face over and over and over again until there was no longer any cries of panic or pain or life.

"I told him," the voice said, breathing heavily. "I told him again and again to obey me."

I'm going to die here.

The thought sprang into Jefferson's mind and the truth of it settled onto his chest. He stopped fighting. He let his arms and legs lie still. He couldn't slow his breathing or stop sobbing but he chose to stop fighting against his bonds.

"I told him and told him and told him," the voice said, growing angry.

Jefferson heard the voice rising as it spoke, returning to a standing posture.

"But did he listen to me?" the voice asked. "No, he didn't."

Jefferson heard the voice's breathing, felt the voice's body lean against the table.

"He wasn't such a good boy after all, was he?" the voice asked, the lips brushing against Jefferson's stubbled cheeks.

He flinched against the touch.

"Will you be a good boy?" the voice asked. "For me?"

Jefferson felt a hand, gentle but firm, move across his forehead into his hair. The hand swept slowly, pushed his hair backward until it met the table then came forward again. He felt thin fingers slip into his hair and massage his scalp as they gently raked his hair backwards again.

"I can be a very forgiving Master," the voice said. "I can make you feel nice."

The fingers traced his hairline then started combing back across his scalp again. The fingers felt so gentle, nurturing. Jefferson felt the voice's other hand snake its way down his chest to his stomach to his crotch.

"If you're a good boy, that is," the voice said. "You have to be a good boy, don't you?"

I'm going to die here. I'm going to die here. Oh God, I'm going to die here.

"Don't you want to be a good boy?"

The hand cupped his testicles then jerked suddenly away. The hand on his head grasped his hair, taking a handful in a quick pull.

"Ah," the voice said, picking up the blade from between Jefferson's legs. "There it is."

The hand on his head relaxed, let the hair fall loosely around the fingers that returned to a gentle massaging.

Jefferson felt the wetness between his asscheeks, blood from his shallow exhales. It was sticky and uncomfortable but he could breathe fully now that the sharp object was gone.

The hands continued teasing his hair, massaging his scalp. He felt the blade of the knife slide across his stomach and dip lightly into his naval.

"Don't you want to be a good boy?" the voice asked. It was made of honey and sugar. It was the reassuring parent speaking. It was the nurturing grandmother prodding her grandson on to bigger and better things.

"Yes," Jefferson whispered, feeling tears spill over his eyelids and run down his cheeks.

"That's right," the voice said, lighter than air. "You're going to be *such* a good boy, aren't you?"

"Yes," Jefferson whispered again, barely able to hear his own voice.

The voice's lip brushed against his cheeks and he felt them plant a ginger kiss there against the wetness of his tears.

"That's a good boy. That's a good boy."

The restraints were removed, one by one. The voice started with the ones at his ankles. Jefferson hadn't realized how much pain they had caused him until he was free. His skin felt bruised and swollen, irritated and itchy. The voice moved up to the strap spanning across his stomach.

"That's a good boy," the voice cooed.

Jefferson tried to lie in perfect supplication. He didn't want to face the same fate as the last good boy.

The restraints around his wrists were removed before the ones across his neck and forehead. Then the hands receded and, though Jefferson felt no restraint holding him in place, he remained still. He still couldn't see. It took a tremendous effort of will not to shoot his hands up to his face and remove whatever covered his eyes.

The voice moved around the table. Jefferson listened to the slow steps, each foot dragging with a soft ruffling in the thick carpet. The voice was making a ticking noise that re-minded Jefferson of the sound some engines make when they're first shut down and beginning to cool.

What do I do?

Jefferson wanted to bolt for the door but he couldn't see. He wouldn't be able to find it and, if he did, he was sure he'd just slam into the wall outside it or, worse, go head over tail into the endless ocean surrounding the boat.

Lie still. Wait for instructions.

The voice circled the table twice more, not speaking, just ticking. The voice stopped just behind Jefferson's head on the beginning of the third lap.

Jefferson tried to slow his breathing and shaking but was only somewhat successful.

The hands were in his hair again, so softly that at first he didn't notice, thought maybe it was the air conditioner quietly moving his hair about.

"We will do great things," the voice whispered, so close to Jefferson's head it could have been resting on the table behind him, "if you're a good boy."

The hands moved slowly, tenderly down his scalp, over the raw and scabbed area where his ears used to be, on down to his stubbled cheeks. The hands rested on his chin, cupping it lightly. Jefferson, unsure whether it was from hearing the end of the last good boy or from some other subconscious sense, was sure he could feel the power radiating in those fingers. He was sure he could feel the well of strength, cached just a hair's width under the surface, waiting for him to slip up, waiting for him to be a bad boy.

The image of a newborn baby flashed into his mind. Bloody, screaming, confused and helpless. The image coupled with that of a slightly larger infant, reaching up and crying, being dipped into a cool, clear body of water.

"Go ahead and sit up," the voice said.

The hands had dissolved from his face without his noticing.

Jefferson rolled forward, jerking with the motion after being forced into a flat position for an extended period of time. He brought his knees to his chest and reached around them to his ankles. They were swollen. The restraints had been far too tight.

"Good," the voice said.

Jefferson moved his hands away from his ankles and checked his wrists, finding the same result.

"Go on and sit on the edge of the table."

Jefferson swung his legs in unison to his left and let them drop off the edge of the table. His movements were staggered and cautious. He didn't want to fall off the table because he couldn't see the end of it.

"There you go," the voice said. "Good boy."

Jefferson forced his hands to rest on his thighs and not move upward to his unseeing eyes. Twice they moved without his conscious calling and he forced himself to slap them back onto his thighs. He hoped the voice would see this as nervous eagerness.

The hands of the voice began to massage his shoulders.

"You're too skinny," the voice said. "We'll have to fix that, won't we?"

The hands kneaded the knots in his back then moved up to his neck.

"And I haven't seen you smile since I laid eyes on you."

Jefferson felt his face twitch.

"Can you smile for me?" the voice asked. "Be a good boy and smile for me?"

He lifted his upper lip and tried to curve the corners. The motion felt foreign. He felt like it'd been years since he last smiled, centuries.

"Close," the voice said. "A little less teeth, at least until we can get you cleaned up."

Jefferson readjusted the muscles of his face until he heard the sounds of approval come from the voice, who'd walked around the table and now stood in front of him, its touch never leaving him.

"That's a good boy," the voice said.

Jefferson heard the dry lip noise of another person smiling. It brought his hands up from his thighs again. He wanted to see the owner of the voice. He needed to see who stood over him.

"Go ahead," the voice told him. "It's OK. Go ahead."

Jefferson lifted his hands again and slowly moved them up to his face. His fingers started with his cheeks and cautiously moved up from there.

"No," he whispered. "No."

"Yes," the voice whispered back. "Yes."

Jefferson felt the thick twine where it entered his skin and followed it across his eyeball to where it exited. It roped back around and over. Again and again.

Sewn shut.

Jefferson began trembling like he hadn't done once in his life up until this point. He dug his fingers into the twine but sharp splinters of pain erupted from his touch and his hands unconsciously shot away.

"Careful now," the voice said. "You'll do more damage than we can fix."

We.

"What have you . . . ?" Jefferson faltered, replaying the final noises of the last good boy in his mind and changed his question. "What's wrong with my eyes?"

The voice's hands lifted from his legs.

"You haven't earned them yet."

He heard the opening and closing of a door off to his right. He remained as still as he could, listening with his hands back on his thighs.

He heard nothing. Just the sound of his own breathing.

He lifted his hands back to his closed eyes. The skin of his eyelids and surrounding areas was thick, swollen. The twine was very rough, almost hemp-like in its consistency.

Jefferson always hated splinters. One of his earliest memories was of screaming his head off until his father open-handed him across the face to bring him to his senses. He'd had a splinter in his left palm and his father had been trying to remove it for nearly ten minutes. Little Jefferson had squirmed and fidgeted under his father's hands, under the little sewing needle and metal tweezers. His father eventually got the thing out but not before having to pop Jefferson to still him.

Jefferson imagined little splinters spiraling across the surface of his eyeballs each time he felt them move against the thick twine.

He let his hands search for the beginning or end of the suture but knew, even if he found it, he couldn't bring himself to remove it. In his mind he saw each movement of the twine against his eye leave a trail of splinters like a half-squashed pregnant spider scampering off, shedding its young.

He felt sick to his stomach and lightheaded. He felt completely drained of any energy he ever had. He let his shoulders slump and felt the trickle of tears wetting the inside of the twine. When his eyes moved against the twine, now moistened with his tears, it felt grainy and silt-like, the riverbed at the start of a flood.

I'm going to die here, he thought.

There're worse things than death.

Jefferson wept.

He hadn't bothered exploring the room. When he'd cried himself stupid and found himself slipping off the table, he swung his legs back up and returned to the position he'd been bound in. He slept.

He woke to darkness. His hands went to his eyes and he found that they were still sewn shut. He'd nearly forgotten, coming from whatever other place he'd been in during his dreams. The rough twine against his fingertips brought him back to his reality.

"Good evening," the voice said.

Jefferson jerked himself fully awake but didn't try to sit up. He carefully, minutely moved each of his legs and found them unbound.

"Feeling rested?" the voice asked. "Good."

Jefferson felt the hands inch under his bare shoulders and lift him into a sitting position.

"You've been such a good boy," the voice told him. "I'm

126

going to give you a little treat."

Jefferson listened to the voice walk back across the room and open the door. He heard the voice say something to someone just on the other side of the door.

He still couldn't tell if the voice was male or female. He couldn't tell by the voice's hands either. This was deeply troubling to Jefferson.

He listened as the door was closed and two sets of feet moved across the room toward him.

"Don't move," the voice told him, stern but still light. "Be a good boy and don't you move an inch."

Someone moved in close and placed one hand behind Jefferson's head, cradling his skull by the top of his neck.

"Don't move," the voice said, from just off to the left. "Be a good boy."

There was a prick at the corner of his left eye.

Jefferson jerked, involuntarily, away from the touch.

"Don't you move," the voice barked. It scared Jefferson how much it'd changed in that instant.

He held perfectly still as the prick came again. It stung as it prodded, followed by a pressure very foreign and nausea inducing. Just when he thought he could take no more, a span of light flooded into his left eye.

It blinded him and he squinted against it.

"Hold really still now," a different voice said.

This voice was very obviously that of a man. It was husked with what sounded like decades of heavy tobacco use.

Jefferson held really still, letting his left eye be prodded. A bit more light flooded in.

He could make out the man's face in front of his. The man was portly, had a full graying beard and half-rimmed glasses. His face was contracted in concentration. His right hand partially obscured his face as he worked on Jefferson's left eye.

"Not too much," the voice said, just off to the left of the

man with the gray beard.

Jefferson turned his eye toward the voice and saw her. She was small, compact and thin. Her head was buzzed down to just the faintest of stubble. Her eyes looked too big for her face. Her lips too full.

The man with the gray beard pinched something and Jefferson squeezed his eye shut with the stabbing of pain.

"Take it back a bit," the woman said.

The man set something down onto the table and picked something else up. Jefferson opened his eye to see the man lean in closer, his tongue poking out the corner of his mouth, teasing a tuft of beard.

Then his narrow line of sight was narrowed even further.

"A little more," the woman said.

Jefferson's vision condensed to a thin line of sight. He could see only the man's bearded chin. He'd have to move his head back to see the rest of his face.

"There," the woman said. "Perfect."

The man with the gray beard pinched something and Jefferson felt tears sting into his eyes, flooding out what little sight he was allowed.

"All right," the man said. "Done."

"Thank you," the woman said. "You may leave us now."

Jefferson made to move his hand up to his eye but the woman's hand slapped onto his wrists before he got close.

"No," she said.

Jefferson didn't know how he couldn't have recognized the voice as belonging to a woman.

"Let me," she said.

She released Jefferson's hand and he let it drop to his lap.

He felt the woman's hands move across his face. He felt her wipe the tears from his eyes.

Somewhere off to the right, the door of the room closed with a faint click.

The woman gently patted away the tears stuck in the small slit between his sewn eyelids.

"There," she said. "Isn't that better?"

Jefferson looked into her face.

"Isn't that better?" she asked again, little strips of metal edging into her voice.

Jefferson found he couldn't look into her eyes. He nodded his head and looked away.

"Come," she said.

Jefferson got down off the table and followed. She opened the door and Jefferson saw the wide hallway, three thick and carved doors facing him from across it, open before him. She stepped through the door and turned, waiting on him.

"Come," she said again.

Jefferson walked through the door and she closed it behind him. He saw, through the narrow slit afforded him, that this door depicted body parts being removed from struggling people.

God.

He looked quickly away from the door. She stood beside him, watching him. The corners of her mouth were curled up in the faintest hint of a smile.

"That's right," she said. "Remotio. You were due for another removal. Lucky for you my last pet turned out to be a disappointment. Disobedient little wretch."

Jefferson turned his gaze toward the floor.

"You don't want to be a disappointment, do you?" she said. "You want to be a good boy, don't you?"

Jefferson nodded his head. His one seeing eye flooded with tears and blurred his vision.

"Come," she said.

Jefferson followed.

She—Jefferson thought of her solely as "She" now—strode

across the hallway, to another of the wide, carved doors. She rested her hand on the door but did not open it right away. Instead, She turned back to Jefferson.

"You will obey me. You will do exactly what I say," She said. "You will not be a disappointment. You will be a good boy."

Jefferson saw no hint of a smile on her face. Her gaze was hard, cold, wrought iron, impenetrable.

Jefferson quickly nodded his head and found it difficult to stop once he had started.

"Good," She said and opened the door.

She disappeared into the darkness inside. Jefferson moved closer to the door, straining to see inside with his one seeing eye. He could make out nothing in the darkness. The room yawned open like a cavern.

Jefferson turned back to the door to study the carving, to get a better idea of what lurked just a few steps inside. The door was illustrated with images of people being strangled. He saw fiendish men and women choking the life out of their victims with horrid smiles painted across their faces. He saw people being hanged from tree branches. He saw people being garroted from behind. He saw one man stepping on a child's throat. The kid's hands were clutched around the man's hairy calves, fingers digging into the bare skin.

Oh God.

"Come," She said from within.

Jefferson stepped into the darkness.

The door was closed behind him. He didn't see anybody there but it was very hard to tell in the darkness.

"Come," She said from straight ahead, "now."

Jefferson took blind, tentative steps forward. He didn't want to trip over anything.

He heard something then. It was faint and because of its

faintness he didn't immediately place the noise. Then he heard it again, a little louder after a few more steps toward She.

It was the same sound he heard from the stairwell in the party house. It was the sound of somebody suffocating.

God.

"Come," She said again, this time from somewhere just to Jefferson's right.

He turned and started that way but something brushed against his face. He jerked away and something light bumped against the back of his head.

Jefferson, flooded with panic, jerked this way and that, each time something unseen in the darkness bumping against his head or his face. He dropped to a crouch.

"Be still," She said.

There was amusement in her voice.

Jefferson wrapped his arms around his knees and shook.

What is this?

There was the sound of plastic ruffling then deep gasps from Jefferson's left. He turned his head and body in that direction but did not stand or move away. He was afraid of what he'd run into, afraid he might hurt himself if he moved.

Deep gulps of air were taken and exhaled, over and over again. Then the crying and pleading started.

"Please, stop," a man's voice said. "Please, for the love of God, stop. I won't tell anyone. Just let me go, please."

She did not respond.

Jefferson pulled his knees tighter, closer to his chest.

The man wept. He cried out in unintelligible pleas for mercy. He spat out similarly non-understandable curses and damnations. After what felt like hours, the man became quiet.

Jefferson did his best to hold still and hush his breathing so he could hear what was happening. The room was nearly pitch black. He could make out nothing with the exception of the faint rectangular outline of the door to the hallway.

"Come," She said.

Jefferson moved without hesitation. He slunk in the direction of She, careful not to rise to a full stand.

There was a click and light flooded the room.

Jefferson shielded his one open eye and crouched further to the floor.

He peered through the spaces between his fingers and scanned the room. She stood three feet to his right, her right hand still on the wall beside the lightswitch she'd just flicked on. Jefferson turned around and saw a table at the center of the room. A naked man was strapped to it. On the floor, at the head of the table, was a plastic grocery bag.

Jefferson looked upwards. Hanging from the ceiling were dozens of nooses, all seemingly made from different material. There were thick nooses and thin nooses, some made from various ropes, others from what looked like piano wire or some other thin metal strand. One appeared to be made from bedsheets.

"Stay," She said, striding past Jefferson toward the table and the naked, restrained man.

Jefferson turned himself to fully face the table and remained where he was.

She bent over and picked up the plastic bag.

Walmart bag, Jefferson thought.

"Please," the man whispered.

She rose and held the bag up over the man's face, showing him the thing.

Tears streamed down the man's face. Spit and snot bubbled. Jefferson saw that the man was missing most of his nose. A crusted wound sat like a sinkhole where it should've been.

Remotio. God.

Jefferson quickly took stock of the rest of the man. He

didn't have a right hand. Just a blood-crusted stump where it should've been. His feet were missing toes. His remaining left hand, fingers.

"Please, lady," the man begged. "Please don't do this."

She slowly, methodically opened the plastic bag and showed the man the inside of it.

"Fuck you!" the man screamed. "Fuck you, you bitch! I'll fucking kill you! Bitch!"

She did not so much as flinch from the sudden violent outburst. She carefully moved the bag around in her steady hands, ensuring the man saw every last centimeter of it.

Then She wrenched the man's head up from the table by a handful of his hair and slipped the bag over his head.

The table jerked with his struggles but the restraints held fast. The man tried to shake his head but She held it firmly to the table by the palms of her right hand.

Jefferson listened to the clomping sound of the man trying to bite down on the bag, to tear a hole through the plastic.

She kept the bag taut across his face with the hand not holding the man's head to the table, ensuring the bag's integrity, keeping the man from biting through the thin plastic.

She looked down at the man struggling under her. Her face was placid, expressionless. Vapid. She could've been any normal person doing some mundane activity, like the dishes or laundry or making a grocery list.

She's killing him.

His mind stated the obvious. He could bring no other thoughts to the forefront of his consciousness.

She's killing him. Right now.

The man's frantic motions began to slow, to grow more labored as his oxygen waned. Just when Jefferson thought the man was dead, She yanked the bag off his head.

The man sucked in air, sputtered, coughed. His bare chest heaved with the effort of filling and refilling his starved lungs.

She turned toward Jefferson. Her eyes were daggers. Hooks sinking into Jefferson. He found he couldn't look away.

"Come," She said.

Jefferson didn't move right away.

Her eyes appeared to flash, to grow even harder.

"Come," She said, lower in volume.

Jefferson made to rise.

"No," She said. "Crawl."

Jefferson dropped to his knees and, moving one hand and one knee at a time, crawled across the room to the head of the table where She waited, watching.

She held the plastic bag in her left hand, her right pressed against the man's forehead, holding his head against the table.

Jefferson stopped crawling and sat back on his haunches at her feet. She kept her eyes locked onto his.

She handed down the bag. Jefferson took it with both of his hands palm up.

"Stand," She said.

Jefferson stood.

The man's sputtering had nearly subsided.

"Who's there?" he asked. "What are you doing?"

"Here," She said, pointing to a spot just behind the head of the table.

Jefferson took the four steps to the spot and stood, waiting for his next command.

She took another handful of the man's hair and jerked his head up off the table.

The man began screaming.

"Bag him," She said.

Jefferson heard the crinkling of the bag in his shaking hands as the man momentarily stopped his screaming to get another mouthful of air.

"Be a good boy," She said. "Bag him."

Jefferson slipped his fingers into the handles of the bag and opened it. He looked inside it. It was glistening with moisture.

"Now," She said.

Jefferson moved the bag forward, seeing the top of the man's head, his black hair coming out like weeds in the sidewalk between She's strong fingers. He slid the plastic bag under the man's head and She moved her hand as he covered the man's head.

"No," the man shouted, somewhere between a plea and a curse.

Jefferson moved his hands forward until they touched the man's naked shoulders, until the top of the man's head, now covered completely in plastic, touched his own chest. When he could stretch the bag no further, he looked to She.

"Good boy," She said. "That's a good boy."

She flicked her head to the wall opposite the door.

Jefferson walked over to the spot and leaned his back against the cold wallpaper. He let gravity pull him down, slowly sliding his back down the wall, until he sat, watching the man struggle to breathe.

She held the man's bagged head down until all of his motion ceased.

"Stop that," She said, turning away from the dead man on the table.

Jefferson, startled, tried to back away but found only wall behind him.

"I said stop that," She said. "There will be no crying. Only little pussies cry. Are you a pussy?"

Jefferson hadn't realized he'd been crying. He quickly sucked air in through his nostrils and held his breath. He wiped the tears and snot from his face with the palms of his hands. He let the air out through his mouth and forced himself to take steady, reasonable breaths.

"Good," She said, turning back to the dead man on the table.

She slowly pulled the bag from the man's head. Jefferson saw that his eyes were wide, unseeing, his mouth agape.

She let the bag slowly float back to the carpet. Jefferson watched it dance its slow path to the floor then lie still as untouched water.

She walked slowly around the table, trailing a hand over the dead man's naked body in her wake. Her face was tranquil. Her eyes were softer than they'd been only a few second before. Her demeanor was that of someone admiring a great work of art.

After She'd made a full circle of the table, her hand caressing the man's body, She stopped back at the head of the table and turned to Jefferson.

"You did well," She said, "my little good boy."

Jefferson felt the smile spread across his face before he could stop it. Then he felt his face flush crimson and he had to look away.

She let him out of the room, the nooses swaying slightly with the unfelt rocking of the boat. Back out in the hallway, Jefferson jumped at the clicking shut of the door behind him.

She allowed him to walk upright in her wake. She took the hall on the left, her long legs carrying her stridently down the smaller hall back toward the cabin barroom. Jefferson couldn't stop himself from sneaking looks at her ass as they went.

She crossed the heavily carpeted cabin room to the bar. She slapped her right palm onto the bar top and, nearly simultaneously, the cabin door opened and a servant entered.

"Yes, ma'am?" he said, crossing the room to the bar.

"Tom Collins," She said.

The servant ducked down behind the bar and came back up with a Collins glass and set about making her drink.

Jefferson fidgeted, unsure what to do with himself.

She turned slightly and looked out the pristinely clear windows at the sunbathers on the deck. Her face was smooth. She could've been any other woman casually waiting for her drink at the bar.

Jefferson had to clamp his mouth shut twice. He felt on the verge of pelting her with questions.

That, surely, is a very bad idea.

Jefferson nodded slightly to himself and resumed looking at his wringing hands.

The servant set the drink down on the bar, on an embroidered cloth napkin, and disappeared out the room down the stairs. She took the drink in her slender, musician-like fingers. The ice in the cup whispered the faintest hint of a rattle. She brought the thin straw to her lips and drank.

Jefferson felt uneasy watching her drink. He, instead, alternated his gaze from his fidgeting hands, to the windows to his left, to the bar ahead and, sidewise, at She, standing at the bar before him.

She drank slowly. Setting the drink down between sips, running her index finger around the lip of the glass in a methodical and steady circle.

Just as She was coming to the end of her drink, the servant appeared at the foot of the steps. Jefferson hadn't heard him ascend. The man stood there, his face turned toward She, his eyebrows upturned in quiet questioning.

She was still facing the window, her back to both Jefferson and the servant.

"Not right now," She said.

The servant nodded, turned and silently descended the stairs back into the belly of the boat.

She took one last sip from the straw and set the glass back on the bar.

Jefferson bounced his weight between his bare feet.

"You did well earlier," She said.

Her back, straight as an arrow, still faced him.

The stray image of grabbing the woman by the nape of her small neck and smashing her head repeatedly into the bar flashed in Jefferson's mind.

She turned so quickly that, with only the limited vision of his half-slitted left eye, Jefferson's mind almost didn't register her movements. One moment she was casually looking out the window, the next she was leaning toward him, her lean, muscular arms crossed under her breasts.

"But I still have my doubts," She said.

Her face was hard. No lines showed up but the skin seemed taut, stretched over a monster's mask nearly to the point of splitting and revealing the horror just underneath.

"You are alive," She said, "thanks to me. Because of me."

She took one slow step toward him.

"You will remain alive," She said, "only because of me."

She seemed to tower over him. Jefferson felt like She had grown two feet in five seconds.

"You are promised nothing," She said. "You are nothing. You are property."

Jefferson cowered away from the monstrous woman. He'd seen the violence She was capable of and She seemed only a hair's breadth away from it now.

"You are no one now. I own you."

She reached down and lifted Jefferson's chin upward, pulling his one open eye into hers.

"Debts and bad pain," She said, lowering her voice. "There is no one here to help you but me."

She left him there in the cabin barroom. She disappeared
138

down the stairs into the belly of the boat. She didn't instruct him to follow, didn't tell him to stay either.

Jefferson thought it was best to stay out of her way for the time being.

He stood where She'd left him for some time, paralyzed with inaction.

What do I do? Where am I supposed to go?

He had no answer for himself.

He wanted to burst out the door onto the deck, grab a life-saver flotation device and leap into the ocean. Face his chances on the open sea away from She and the horrors of this yacht.

He also wanted to go behind the bar and pour alcohol into himself until he died.

Instead, Jefferson carefully made his way to the couch against the wall on the far side and sat down. He slowly, wary of harm, something sharp or dangerous hidden in the folds of the thing, leaned back until his neck no longer supported his head. He tried to keep his eye open but found it exponentially increasing in weight.

Jefferson drifted off into sleep.

He was at the party, in the house, out somewhere in the middle of eastern Kentucky's nowhere. He was running through the long, echoing halls completely naked, splattered in blood. He was laughing, tears streaming down his eyes, making little peach riverbeds down his crimson cheeks.

"You can't run," a voice playfully called from behind. "There's nowhere to go."

Jefferson felt giddy, his head light on his shoulders, his bare feet slapping the floor with an unsteadiness not unlike being completely shitfaced. Gurgled laughter bubbled up his throat, spilled out of his open mouth.

The hall was coming to an end. There was a blotchy face

painted in thick, crusty oils hanging on the wall in front of him. Jefferson came to the end and stared into the face. It looked strangely familiar, somebody he knew but couldn't quite place.

He heard the slow, steady footfalls behind.

A smile spread across his face but his stomach dropped. He made to turn around and time condensed, slowed to a near standstill.

He couldn't whip his head around and get a glance of his pursuer. His body felt crystalline, inflexible. He heard the steps, louder now, echoing in the nearly empty hall, popping like a loosened snare drum.

"There's nowhere to go, Jefferson."

His body began to spin slowly around, away from the face staring down at him from the frame on the wall. The smile hurt his face but he couldn't make it go away.

"You are not in control. You never will be."

The colors of the hall blurred. Jefferson's body swiveled on a fixed axis. He turned and saw that the hall stretched out further than any hall in reality could. It went on and on and on until his vision gave out and a vague haziness supplanted sight.

A dark figure crouched before him. There was no skin, no sex identifiable features.

It spoke again.

"Debts and bad pain, Jefferson. You'll never be free."

Jefferson's body glided toward the crouched figure. He tried to reach out, leech his fingernails into the walls to stop himself from nearing it.

It rose smoothly and with a grace unlike anything Jefferson had ever seen. Its stature was immense. Its head, once fully standing, hung just centimeters under the high ceiling.

Jefferson was lifted upwards.

"Debts and bad pain."

A face flickered into life in the darkness of the figure's head.

Jefferson stared smiling into a reflection of himself, some nine feet off the ground.

He woke with a start, an unseen hand having seemingly shaken him awake. He jerked up from the couch and squinted into the darkness of the cabin barroom with his half-opened left eye.

Night had come and flooded the world with darkness. Not one light was on inside the room. There was no one, that Jefferson could see, in the room either.

He walked across the soft carpet to the window and looked out onto the deck, its surface glittering with the diamond-like light of the pregnant moon overhead. He stared out, slowing his breathing and coming fully to his senses.

He had the feeling he just woke from a monster of a bad dream but couldn't remember anything other than a hallway.

He carefully, cautiously rubbed his slitted left eye with the palm of his hand. Crust flecked off and powdered his cheek.

Something flittered across the deck, moving quickly and stealthily.

He leaned forward, his forehead pressing against the glass, to get a better look.

It stopped at the foot of the metal stairs on the other side of the deck.

Jefferson couldn't make it out.

He opened the cabin door and stepped out into the night.

He crossed the deck, the steady night breeze rushing against his body, pressing his servant's clothing against his goosepimpled skin.

"Hello?" he half-whispered.

No answer but the wind.

He picked up his pace and jogged by the empty sun chairs

and tables. The shape darted up the stairs. Jefferson followed.

He crested the stairs and a thin, ghostlike man stood waiting. He, too, was dressed as a servant.

Jefferson and the man stood there, looking at each other, for several tense moments.

The man didn't have an ounce of extra weight on him. His face was barely more than a skull with skin. His eyes sunk impossibly far into their sockets, his lips not really lips but just places where the skin of his face ended and the hole of his mouth began.

Jefferson stepped closer to better see with his one eye.

The man had no ears. The skin was gnarled but fully healed in the places where they should have been. Thick, purpled scar tissue ran the length of his eyes, both above and below.

"You'll never escape," the man said.

His voice was harsh, barely human sounding, but not much louder than a library whisper. The sound of a glass gurgler or someone who'd drunk acid or had throat cancer.

"Who are you?" Jefferson asked.

"It doesn't matter," the man said. "I'm no one. Like you."

The man was missing most of the fingers on both of his hands.

"What are you talking about?" Jefferson asked.

"They'll never let you go," the man said. "You're better off dead."

"You're crazy," Jefferson whispered.

The man shook his head.

"Maybe," he said, "maybe not. It doesn't matter. I used to be like you."

Jefferson recalled his own reflection in the servant's mirror deep in the bowels of the boat. He shook his head at the emaciated man, a strange mixture of anger, fear and hostility rising in his sour stomach.

"I'm nothing like you."

"Not yet, maybe, but you will be. There is no escape. Debts and bad pain, debts and bad pain."

The man repeated the phrasing over and over again, like a mantra.

"What is that?"

"Debts and bad pain, you're no one now. It's better to die."

The man turned away from Jefferson in one quick motion and leapt over the railing. Jefferson watched the man's silent, screamless fall. He hadn't pushed outward enough to avoid the yacht's deck railing some twenty feet below. His body smacked off it, crumpled over and splashed into the dark silent water. The force of the fall and the sound of the man's frail body splintering against the thick metal railing sent a wave of shivers up Jefferson's spine.

I'm going to die here, he thought without any conscious effort. *Oh, God, I'm going to die here.*

Jefferson squinted down, hanging over the rail for a better look, but didn't see the man in the water below. It was too dark or he'd already sank, escaping from what terror he'd known. The water sent up a refracted reflection of the full moon, glittering and swaying with constant motion.

Jefferson looked up from the dark water at the deep blue of the sky above. Stars shone their constant swan song, dotting the night sky with pinpricks of light. The moon looked close enough to reach up and touch. He stared up into the pale face of it and felt the tears slowly find their way through the thick twine of his sewn up right eye and down onto his cheeks. His left eye blurred over and the moon was lost in a smear of white, black and gray.

She woke him. A quick burst of shaking from a strong hand. He'd been curled up in a tight little ball on the couch in the

143

cabin barroom, where he'd cried himself into a restless slumber some time before.

"Wake up," She said.

Jefferson had to remove crusted gunk from his eye before he could see. He did this as fast as he could but careful so as to not trap any of the stuff inside his half-lidded eye.

He sat up and saw that She was wearing a one-piece bathing suit. It was red and very tightly fitted.

I thought only fat chicks and moms wore one-piece suits, was his first thought of the day.

"Can you swim?" She asked.

Jefferson nodded his head and stood.

"Good," She said. "Come."

He followed her out into the early morning sunshine. Thick clouds billowed off in the horizon but it could've been miles and miles away for all Jefferson could tell.

There were sunbathers out on the deck but not as many as yesterday. Jefferson assumed many were not awake yet.

This is one fucked up cruise, he thought. *You can torture and murder people whenever you like then catch some rays.*

Jefferson clipped one of her sandals with his foot and nearly fell.

She turned around with the celerity of a cat.

"Pay attention," She spat.

She reached down and readjusted the sandal on her right foot.

Jefferson shrank away from her. The sounds and mental depiction of her last good boy being pummeled to death came rushing back to him. He came to full waking nearly instantaneously.

She swung back around and marched on. Jefferson followed but at a greater distance than before.

Most of the sunbathers out were older. Several appeared to be in their fifties, most younger but not by much.

144

Semi-retired serial killer cruises? I picture that being a real bitch to market.

Jefferson's eye rolled over the bare, sagging chest of a heavily tanned woman sprawled on one of the chairs to the coastline just visible behind. It stopped him in mid-step.

Holy shit, he thought. *Land.*

He stepped over to the railing, in between two snoozing sunbathers, and squinted off into the distance. He could just make out the thick green of trees and foliage. He saw the gold and white glittering reflection of sandy beaches. He did not see one single man-made structure. Not a house or a hotel or a road. He scanned the water around it and did not find another boat or watercraft.

"Come," She demanded.

Her voice spiked through him like a lobotomy pick. He jerked away from the railing as if it were hot. He nearly fell onto a fat, gray-bearded man clad only in a navy blue thong asleep in one of the chairs.

Jefferson regained his balance and trotted across the deck to where She stood waiting, hands on hips, foot tapping.

"I do not like to repeat myself," She said once he was panting at her feet.

Jefferson opened his mouth to apologize but she shot out a hand to stop him.

"I did not say you could speak," She said.

Jefferson clapped his mouth shut.

"We're going for a swim. I feel like exercising."

She kicked off her sandals and motioned for Jefferson to undress.

"It looks further than it is," She said, flicking her head toward the coast. "It can't be more than sixteen-hundred meters. A nice warm up for what I've got waiting for us once we get there."

A smile, as lurid as an exposure, crept across her face. It

145

made Jefferson's own flush hot and red. He slipped out of his unbuttoned shirt and undid the fastening on his slacks. She watched him, her smile firmly in place.

Jefferson realized he wasn't wearing any underwear and hesitated.

"Come now," She said, smiling. "I think we're beyond that, aren't we?"

Jefferson let the pants drop to his ankles, the sun bearing down on his naked body. He made to cup himself but She shook her head.

"Enough of that frivolity. You have no privacy."

She turned, swung one leg over the railing, then the other, and dove, arms extended, hands together as if in prayer, into the ocean. It was in a league of gracefulness in stark contrast to the servant's awkward freefall from a few hours earlier.

Jefferson watched her smooth strokes as she made her way toward shore and knew he would keep her waiting for some time if he didn't follow her immediately. He climbed over the railing and belly flopped into the cold, salty water.

It took his breath away. He'd meant to dive but, only having one eye, and it only partially open, his depth perception was off. He'd meant to arc his dive and get the most distance away from the boat before curving his body downward and entering the water in a more linear fashion.

He came up sputtering and splashing. His legs kicked fiercely under him until he regained his breath. He could just make out the treeline off in the distance, when the rolling water descended its crest. He started off, doing his best to conserve his energy yet not keep her waiting.

Swimming does something to a body. Its very regulated and constant motion focuses all of one's faculties to the task at hand. Jefferson's wounds, completely bathed in the stinging saltwater, sung out in pain but he was able to ignore them.

He slowed his stroke periodically to gauge his course. Eventually, he fell into looking up every thirty strokes.

His mind emptied itself while his body worked. Scenes from the past several days played out in fast-forward-like skipping. He saw the party, Caerulean, his ponygirl, buttplug tail in place, eyes open but unseeing. He saw the forest path in the growing morning, the stumps where his fingers were supposed to be. He saw the bodies on the couches. He saw the body at the top of the stairs. The house on fire. He saw the woman in the room of monitors. He saw the servants and the eighteen-year, the bourbon. He saw the smiling man and the woman in the valley.

Jefferson saw all of this in single, cycling clips. He saw them but did not process them. He was growing tired from the swim and took to doing just enough to keep himself propelling forward.

He looked up and saw the shore, much nearer now. She was standing on the beach, the sharp bristles of her closely cropped hair shining in the sun.

He went back to swimming and picked up his pace. He worked at it for some time and only realized he'd made it when his belly scraped the bottom. He let his legs drop, his toes sinking into the silky sand, and stood, hunched over and breathing heavily.

"Come," She called from the beach.

Jefferson trudged toward the shore, his hands clasped together over his head to better allow oxygen into his lungs.

She watched him come.

He made it onto the shore and turned around. The boat, massive and yawning, was a little white blip on the still horizon.

"You did well," She said.

Jefferson turned around and made his way up the slight incline where She stood.

They walked along the beach, in silence, for nearly half an hour. Sweat beaded then dropped and ran freely in little rivulets across Jefferson's body.

She did not appear to be even remotely fatigued.

He walked to her right, a few steps behind, the ocean on his right. The treeline was unobstructed for as far as he could see. It was a tangled mess of trees and vines and bushes. Jefferson, nearly completely unknowledgeable in regards to botany, wasn't able to place any of the plant life.

I have no idea where we are, he thought.

The boat receded further and further as they walked until Jefferson could no longer make it out in the blue-on-blue of the ocean horizon.

"We're almost there," She said. "You're breathing quite heavily."

Jefferson did his best to quiet his breathing. It was hard. He tried breathing only through his nostrils but found he couldn't get enough air this way. He took to turning his head slightly away from her, toward the ocean, when he exhaled.

"Do you still have thoughts of your own?" She asked.

The question nearly stopped him in his tracks.

What's that supposed to mean?

"Ah," She said, nodding at the expression Jefferson hadn't intended to be visible. "That'll change. Soon enough, that'll change."

Jefferson did his best to make his face formless, opaque.

"We lost another debtor last night," She said.

He didn't understand at first. Then Jefferson recalled the servant's fervent declarations of hopelessness and his awkward plummet into the ocean came to his mind.

Debtor, he thought. *I, too, am a debtor then.*

"You wouldn't happen to know anything about this?" She asked.

148

Jefferson saw her looking at him as She walked. There was another smile on her face, this one knowing and playful.

Jefferson was still trying to form an answer when she stopped him.

"Of course you do," She said. "There truly isn't any other escape than death."

His mind was painfully empty. His body moved but felt like vacant cornhusks flickering in the nighttime air on a late harvest wind.

"Ah," She said, "we're here."

A small path, unmarked by anything except its opening, led into the woods.

She took Jefferson by the wrist, her hand cold to the touch, and pulled him along, kicking up sand before them. The sand gave way to hardened, packed dirt as the path went. It was just wide enough for one person to walk comfortably but She didn't let go of Jefferson's wrist so he stumbled along bushes, roots and ferns lining the path.

"The mind, the ego, the sense of the self, is pliable," She said.

Jefferson wondered how she wasn't even breathing hard.

"It's a product of the society, the structures and substructures of hierarchy, in which one lives."

He couldn't hear the ocean anymore. The absence of its constant, yet somehow always background, speaking heightened his growing alarm.

"You, a once relatively powerful and respected member of society, are now nothing," She said. "You have no society. You have no power. No worth. And soon you will have no sense of self."

She was watching him out of the corner of her eye as she spoke.

Jefferson's face twitched with the effort of keeping it blank.

What is this? Where is she taking me?

"Your sense of self, your ego, will die. It is dying now. You are in a mourning phase for it, for the person you used to be. Don't worry, it will pass. You will accept who you are, no one, soon enough."

What is she talking about?

"Or you will perish," She said, letting go of his wrist.

Jefferson dropped back, allowing her to pass forward enough for him to step onto the path. He felt his pulse beating out a painful syncopation in his hand. He looked down at his wrist and, in a ray of light falling through the trees overhead, he saw that it was bruised, swollen, from her grip. His hand was a ghostly blue from the deprivation.

He wondered how he hadn't even felt the pain of her stranglehold.

"Come," She called over her shoulder from the path ahead.

Jefferson fell into a jog to catch up.

The path was a curving, winding thing, weaving between trees growing in height the further into the forest they went. Birds called periodically, squawking alarms that spread the word of their arrival, ahead and around them.

"You will conform to the person allowed you," She said, "or you will die. It's that simple."

Allowed me?

"Either way, the person you thought you were, the name and idea your parents gave you, the sense of power and wealth your job gave you, the individuality you've taken for granted, is dead. Gone. You are no more," She said.

I am not dead, he thought. The thought's voice sounded surprisingly weak though.

The path ahead was shrouded in a hazy shaft of sunlight.

"We're almost there," She said. "It's best you put all of

that out of your mind, for the present. We have work ahead of us."

She stepped through the slit of light and, for a moment, disappeared in the luminance of the blinding sun. Jefferson hesitated, unable to see what awaited him.

"Come," She demanded, still unseen from somewhere ahead.

Jefferson stepped out of the forest into a brightness that dazzled him. He couldn't force his left eye to remain open, it was so bright.

"Follow the sound of my voice," She said.

Jefferson took small, hesitant steps toward her. The ground was absolutely smooth. It felt slick under his feet and Jefferson was afraid he'd slip and crash down at any moment.

"Come," She said again, her voice a little further away this time.

Jefferson took larger steps until the ground under his feet began to slope downward. The dirt and sand did not help with traction. Despite his every best effort, he began to slide forward, down the slope.

It was gradual at first. He shot his arms out to balance himself and remained on his feet. But as the angle of the slope increased, he overcorrected the swinging of his arms and dropped painfully onto his back.

He slid silently, too unnerved to even scream or call out, until the slope mellowed out and he came to rest, shaking and huffing.

He curled up within himself, knees to chest, arms wrapped around shins. He rolled over onto his side but the light, still absolutely blinding, seemed to intensify nearer to the ground. He shifted onto his back and force lifted the lid of his left eye until he could make out the brilliantly blue sky above. He held his eye open until he could stand the brightness and keep his eye open on his own.

He moved his vision around slowly. He could make out the tops of the forest surrounding him. It appeared to Jefferson that he was in a very deep crater of some sort, a hundred feet down or more. He tried to slide his gaze down from the tops of the trees to the edges of the crater but the glare was too bright. The ground appeared to be made of a spotlight, a thousand suns shining up, forcing the eye away.

"It is best if you keep your eyes, or should I say eye, to the sky," She said.

She was very near. Jefferson jerked his head in her direction, instantly blinded by the brightness of the ground surrounding him.

"The sky," She said.

When Jefferson opened his eye, her head was looming over him like a planetoid or some other celestial body. Her face was completely lit, despite the fact that the sun hung somewhere above and behind her, a fact that went fundamentally against all Jefferson had experienced in all of the sunny days of his past.

"Now, orient yourself," She said, her head moving out of his view as she stepped away.

Jefferson kept his eye on the sky above as he slowly sat up. He had to keep his chin jutted up, his neck straining to keep his train of sight above the treeline surrounding the crater, as he put his hands behind him and hoisted himself up.

"Good," She said.

Jefferson nearly lowered his chin to look at her but stopped himself just in time.

"What is this pla—"

Jefferson was struck, hard, just under his sewn up right eye. His head jerked to the left, his neck cracking loudly from the awkward angle. He teetered, taking several steps backward in quick succession, but did not fall.

152

"I did not say you could speak," She said.

Jefferson opened his mouth to apologize but caught himself and snapped it shut again.

His pulse beat in a growing knot on his right cheekbone.

"You must obey," She said.

Jefferson nodded, his neck popping again with the sudden motion, shutting his left eye to avoid being blinded by the shining ground.

"Now," She said, "you will do exactly as I say, when I say it. It won't be long now."

Jefferson kept his head leaned back on his neck, his one open eye on the cloudless blue above him. Time passed very slowly. They waited in silence. He heard nothing but the faint stirring of the branches and leaves of the trees that were very distant from where he stood.

He wanted to sit or lie down. It would be easier to lie on his back, his neck able to rest from the strain of the weight of his head held in the furthest back position he could manage. He didn't lie or sit though. If his right eye hadn't been sewn shut, Jefferson knew he still wouldn't be able to use it after that blow. He tested it with the fingers of his right hand and found it taut and nearly the size of a baseball.

God, She can punch, he thought. *I've never known a woman this strong.*

A bird drifted lazily on some jet stream high above. It was white and very small amidst the gigantic backdrop of the sky. It reminded Jefferson of his last glance at the yacht floating some undeterminable distance off the shore. He wondered how big that bird really was or if, perhaps, it was a rather small bird and much nearer than he thought.

I don't know anything anymore, he thought. *I don't know where I am. I don't know who I'm with. I can't tell how many days I've been gone. I can't tell whether or not that is a gigantic bird flying very high above or just a gull somewhere marginally high. What's happening to me?*

"It's time," She said.

It'd been nothing but silence and the sounds of the forest for so long that he jumped at the sound of her voice. A muscle in his neck twanged painfully and he had to squeeze his left eye shut as his neck refused to hold his head up until the spasm passed.

From somewhere above, off to his right, Jefferson heard voices. One was alarmed, yelling and demanding, several others were joined together in what sounded eerily like Gregorian chanting.

"You will do exactly as I say," She said.

He could tell from the sound of her voice she too was facing the noise.

There was a smacking sound, bare skin being slapped is what it sounded like to Jefferson, then a panicked screaming growing louder and nearer. Someone had been forced down the shining slope. The screams rose to a crescendo and a whisper of it seemed to come from all around Jefferson. It felt like the ghost of the man's screams were bouncing around in the crater like a feedback loop.

Jefferson scooted away in quick little steps until She hissed at him to stay.

He stopped, his neck still straining upward, seeing nothing but blue—the bird had drifted away while he was distracted—and waited. The chanting voices grew nearer as they too made their way down the slope.

"I can't see," the panicked voice, obviously male, shrieked. "What the fuck? I can't see."

The chanting stopped but Jefferson could hear sliding noises and the others' breathing as they approached.

"Stay away from me!" he yelled.

Jefferson listened to the sound of the man's flailings, the slap of his hands or bare feet on the slick, bright ground as he

154

tried to flee his pursuers.

He doesn't even know we're down here, Jefferson thought.

The scampering noises neared and Jefferson knew She was going to strike at any moment. His nerve endings felt electrified knowing what this poor man did not. One part of him wanted to call out a warning, "No! Don't come this way! *She*'s here! She'll kill you just the same as they will!" But another part of him, the part slowly coming to the forefront of his thoughts and actions, kept him still, kept him waiting.

Jefferson shook with nervousness.

"Get away from me!" the man yelled.

The chanting picked up again. Jefferson could hear it rise as the chanters rose to their feet after their slide down the shining slope. Goosebumps broke out across Jefferson's skin. It was such an otherworldly sound, the chanting. Unlike anything he'd ever heard.

"Stop it!" the man screamed. "Leave me alone! Get away from me!"

Jefferson couldn't make out what they were chanting, at first. Slowly, it dawned on him what the mixed voices were saying and a fresh wave of gooseflesh bristled across his body and a shiver went the length of his spine.

"Debts and bad pain," they chanted. "Debts and bad pain."

Jefferson heard the crunch of flesh and bone being struck. The man had just taken in a gulping breath of air, probably preparing to let loose another vain cry for amnesty, then She hit him.

Jefferson wasn't sure how he knew it was her that got to the man but he did.

He heard the man crumple and slap down onto the shining ground. The chanting stopped. The wind tickled Jefferson's sweating forehead, tousling the hair matted there. He wanted to back away, run as far and as fast as he could in any direction away from her and these people, debts and bad pain.

But he stood there, shaking and waiting.

"Here," a voice said.

"Thank you, Richard," She said.

"Should've waited for us," Richard said. "Shouldn't've come down here blind with *him*."

Jefferson kept his eyes to the sky. Somewhere in the background of his mind, he remembered a Richard—even found himself acknowledging that Richard had a different voice from the one currently speaking—but it was a hazy recollection, something seen from a vantage point so far removed to preclude any real recognition of detail.

"Needed a swim," She said.

There was the sound of cloth being ripped and a faint moaning.

Jefferson couldn't see what was happening but pictured it in his mind. The unconscious man's clothes were being ripped off him. He pictured the chanters and She wearing thick lensed goggles or sunglasses to allow them to function on the blinding surface.

"Come," She said.

Jefferson took small, careful steps toward her voice. He reached out his right foot searchingly before setting it down and dragging his left foot even. He repeated the process, his left eye still facing the sky, until he felt naked flesh with his searching right foot and stopped.

"Here," She said.

Something was thrust onto his face. The world darkened and the shapes of spectral people came into view.

She was holding a pair of dark goggles over his face. There was a crumpled, naked man seemingly floating at their feet, surrounded by six other people, four men and two women.

The ground below their feet was a blowing, surfaceless orb. It was exactly what Jefferson pictured the surface of the sun to look like.

A fresh wave of sweat broke out across his body. He felt the heat emanating up from the shining ground.

Jefferson made to take hold of the goggles but She slapped his hand away and continued to hold the goggles in place.

"See," She said.

Jefferson saw that they were indeed in a crater of sorts. It appeared the entire surface of the crater had been covered with glass or some shining metal until it was a gigantic reflector of the sun. He moved his disabled eye as far as he could to see as much as he could. There didn't appear to be anything but the slope.

How the fuck are we going to get out of this place?

He remembered trying to climb steep, metal slides as a child with wet feet. It was a laughably futile thing. Something people videotaped and sent into *America's Funniest Home Videos*.

The world was suddenly sent into a blinding whiteness.

She had jerked the goggles away.

Jefferson squeezed his left eye shut and covered his face with his hands. He saw the negative impression, an undeveloped picture, of the last thing his eye saw before the goggles were removed. Dark, ghastly faces with blackened goggled eyes staring at him. The goggles stretched the appearance of eyes to an alien or demonic shape. The faces were hard. Appraising. A hunger for violence as visible as the sky above.

"Sky," She commanded.

Jefferson craned his head back on his neck and squinted up into the blue.

"I don't see the point of having him—" Richard started but She interrupted.

"Of course you don't," She snapped. "It is none of your

concern. Let us proceed."

Jefferson felt every bit the child listening to his parents argue.

There was the sound of motion. One of the men grunted. Jefferson pictured the naked and unconscious man being hoisted up onto the shoulder, fireman's carry-style, of one of the larger chanters.

Where are they taking him? There's nowhere to go.

They moved around and behind Jefferson. He cringed away from them and waited for a strike that didn't come. He turned his body to follow them as they passed, his eye still on the sky. They didn't move all that far, maybe twenty or twenty-five feet if Jefferson's hearing was even remotely accurate, but it seemed to take them a long time to get there.

Jefferson heard the smack of the naked man being dumped unceremoniously back onto the slick, shining surface. It seemed to echo in the crater and Jefferson wondered again how far he could trust his senses.

"Come," She called, her tone oddly high and resonant.

It sounded small at first then grew and grew, seemed to bounce off the slopes around them and flow back into itself.

Jefferson moved toward the spot where her call initiated. It seemed to be bouncing all over the place now and, if he hadn't been paying close attention, it would've been easy to walk in circles chasing it.

He walked cautiously, his head cocked upward and to the right, leading with his left ear. He walked for a long time, much longer than he would've guessed possible without meeting an edge of the crater. She's command, "Come," was still pinballing around, clouding his senses.

He felt their movements more than heard them and stopped. The chanters were chanting again. It was low, nearly a whisper, and somehow didn't refract off the walls of the crater like She's call.

158

What is this place? Jefferson wondered. *Who are these people?*

There was a zipper noise and something flapped in the light breeze. She's call stopped echoing and an eerie quietness prevailed. Her demand had been bouncing around for so long that, despite the chanting, the crater felt pregnant with its absence.

"Debts and bad pain," they said.

It was oddly tonal. Jefferson knew it could be transplanted at any point in the past two hundred years and still sound old, archaic. If he didn't know English, they could've been saying anything. Jesus Christ, the Redeemer. Lucifer, the Adversary. All Hail the Fallen Angel. Praise Be His Name. It just sounded all encompassing. It was a sweeping noise that, despite its relatively low volume, seemed to swoon once you picked up on it and really focused in.

What has this man done? Jefferson wondered. *What did he do to deserve this?*

The flapping noise stopped.

The chanting began to rise in pitch. Jefferson heard She join in.

There was the noise of hands working. The man remained unconscious and Jefferson could just make out the sound of his breathing amongst the chanting.

"Ready," a woman's voice said.

Someone got up and moved away from the group, off to Jefferson's right. He could tell by the slapping sound they, too, were barefooted. They walked for some time, their steps growing harder and harder to focus on with the chanting so near. Then the steps returned, paused momentarily, and went off in the exact opposite direction. They returned again and went off behind Jefferson. Then returned again and went off some distance ahead of Jefferson.

The steps returned one last time and the chanting jumped up another step in pitch. It was nearing the same tone She had called out to Jefferson in the few moments prior.

"Debts and bad pain," they chanted. "Debts and bad pain."

The man stirred. He moaned. He slowly came to.

"Wha—"

"Debts and bad pain."

"What the fuck?"

"Debts and bad pain."

"Hey!" the man shouted. "What the hell? Untie me, you freaks! Untie me!"

"Debts and bad pain."

Jefferson heard the sound of a camera's click. Someone was snapping photos.

"Let me go you freaks!" the man's voice cracked. The urgency was now fully panic, terror. His bravado was gone.

"Debts and bad pain."

"Now," a woman's voice said.

There was the sound of rope being pulled taut. The man howled in wordless agony.

"Debts and bad pain."

Oh my God.

"Stop it!" the man screamed. "Please!"

"Again," the woman said.

There was the sound of joints popping then a sound eerily similar to a violin string being wound too tightly on the tuning pegs.

The blue of the sky, the sun moving off somewhere behind him over the forest and the beach beyond, looked down almost in mockery. It seemed unmoved to the suffering, the pain, the torture, underneath it.

Tears again welled up in Jefferson's eyes. He couldn't remember the last time he'd cried so much in his life. Not when his mother died. Not when he didn't get the merit scholarship he was positively sure was a lock.

160

The blue sky blurred in his left eye and he felt the snot streaking down his upper lip into his open mouth.

"I'll do whatever you want!" the man screamed. "Just stop it! Please!"

The chanting, as if cued by the man's pleas, rose up another step and the words began to bounce around off the crater's shining surface. Echoing and echoing, the different voices melded together and became one. One voice that came from all sides, at different times. A profusion of malice. A stalking chorus in surround sound.

"Debts and bad pain."

"Finish it," the woman said.

Something already impossibly taut was pulled even tighter, singing for a few seconds as it quivered with vibration.

The man inhaled sharply, followed by an extended groan. The sound you make when you can no longer care for appearance. The sound you make when you consider only making it through.

Then a snapping sound unlike anything Jefferson had heard.

He was slapped up the entire front of his body. His face, neck, chest, arms, nearly every bit of his frontside was splattered with hot liquid. He flinched away, darkened redness blinking out the blue sky, and fell back onto the shining surface.

Jefferson scrambled backward and away, using his bare, sweating arms to wipe his face. He felt the liquid smear. It was thicker than water and warm.

Oh God.

He switched to the palm of his left hand, moving enough of the blood to uncover his slitted left eye. He opened his eye, not to the sky, but to the scene in front of him. The brightness of the shining slope was made visible.

The chanters, who'd ceased chanting after the great pulling apart, stood around a naked torso. The naked man had no arms or legs. Blood, more black than red with the shining surface surrounding it, covered the man, the chanters and a good portion of the ground around them.

Jefferson saw the trail he left on his scampering to where he now cowered. He looked down at his body. He was coated in the man's blood.

Four trails lead away from the limbless man. Jefferson followed the man's right arm's trail and saw it, wrist tied to a blackened rope, some fifteen feet away. There were little posts at four spots around the bottom of the crater. They had notches where the ropes were tied.

Quartered.

Jefferson saw the expression on the man's face. His eyes, now unseeing, were filled with horror and agony. His mouth hung only partly opened. His face was splattered in his own blood.

A high, sweeping noise filled the crater. Like her call and the chanting near the bloody climax, it seemed to echo and bounce off all sides of the crater at once.

Jefferson didn't know where it was coming from until all the chanters and She turned to him. By then, though, he couldn't stop his screaming.

She stomped across the blood, splashing it around under the baking sun, to where Jefferson crouched, screaming in a voice he hadn't known he possessed. Her hand was fast, much quicker than he could see. She open handedly slapped him once. It was enough.

Jefferson's whole body was rocked onto his side from the blow.

He stopped screaming.

When he opened his eye again he had to squeeze it shut right away. He was blinded by the shining surface untouched by the dead man's blood. He rolled over onto his back and blinked up at the sky.

"Control yourself," She hissed down at him.

Jefferson saw the faint outline of a fading jet stream. A plane, piloted by someone unknown, someone a world above the carnage and death surrounding Jefferson. They probably saw nothing but coastline. Sandy beaches and gently breaking waves just off the shore. Maybe a blinding little bright spot, just off the coast in a wooded area. They'd probably think it was a shed. Or a pool reflecting the light of the sun.

They probably didn't even notice, he thought.

"Get up," She said.

Jefferson slowly rose, slipping once in the thickening blood around him.

A man's voice began to speak.

"I don't see why—"

She cut him off.

"No," She snapped, "you don't. And it's not of your concern."

The man didn't offer a response.

Jefferson kept his head craned upward, his eyes on the sky and the last little white trail from the plane, now long gone.

"Gather his limbs," She said.

Jefferson swallowed. His throat felt coated in cotton. His windpipe insufferably narrowed. The motion hurt and brought fresh tears to his eyes.

"Here," She said.

Jefferson's right hand was lifted and something was thrust into it. It was cold and metal.

"Take these and get it done," She demanded.

Something made of cloth was pressed into his left hand.

Jefferson didn't move his eyes from the sky for a moment. He watched as the last of the jet stream melted into the blue of the sky. Gone.

"Do not disappoint me," She whispered.

He could hear the words and the daggers underneath them. He heard them very close to the spot where his right ear should've been. She pressed them through her clenched teeth.

Malice.

Jefferson looked down from the sky and squinted at the surrounding brightness. He saw She'd placed a folding knife in his right hand and a thick, cloth tote bag in his left.

Her face was inches away from his, shining red, the reflection of the crater enhancing the crimson of the man's blood. She no longer wore the goggles and her eyes seemed very black. They burned into Jefferson's one opened eye. Her face, smooth before being covered in another's blood, seemed extra smooth, almost reptilian or shell-like.

She took Jefferson by the shoulder and turned him toward the man's left leg, some distance off to his left. The trail of blood led to where it sat, inches away from the post it was tied to. The jumble of rope lying around it looked like a waiting snake.

She shoved him. Jefferson stumbled before walking carefully to avoid stepping in the trail of blood.

He heard a murmur of voices behind him and knew they were discussing him.

What are they saying?

His legs felt foreign, loaned to him like a borrowed car or another's shoes. He forced one foot in front of the other until he was there, standing over the thing. It was a leg. A man's leg. Just sitting there. Unattached. The hair on the leg moved slightly with the light breeze that swept into the shining crater.

This isn't real.

Jefferson could feel their eyes on him. He knew he had to reach down and pick the thing up, the leg. The unattached leg of a dead man.

A man who was alive not five minutes ago.

Jefferson felt the knife in his hand and let the tote bag drop. He unfolded the knife, using both of his hands, then walked over to the post. It was retractable. It had come up from the ground. He saw where the rope had been tied into it. He saw that, as the post rotated, the rope was wrapped very tightly around it. It was mechanical.

Somewhere there is a motor that turns the thing on and it turns and turns and turns until . . .

Jefferson reached down and felt the rope. It could've been a climber's rope. He let his hand find the bit of the rope descending from the post and used the knife to saw it.

It took some doing. The rope was very well-made.

He then turned to the leg, which he'd been avoiding looking at. It still looked so real.

This isn't real.

It looked like it could be attached to his own body, starting just under his hip and extending to the ground below him.

He reached down and gently picked it up by the ankle. He was surprised at how heavy it was.

This isn't real.

He wanted it to weigh nothing or next to nothing. He wanted it to feel plastic, fake.

It didn't.

He knelt down and opened the cloth tote bag and dropped the leg into it. He gathered up the blood-slick rope and shoved it into the bag too.

He rose, heard his knees pop, and turned back around. The chanters, She included, stood there, watching him. Some of them still wore the goggles, others did not. It was much easier to see with the blood coating the shining surface. Their faces and clothes were also spattered in blood.

Jefferson walked, following beside but not on the blood

trail. He traced it back to the dismembered man, skirted around the group, and went along the next trail to the man's other leg.

This is not real.

He cut the rope from the post and opened the bag for the leg. It peeled open slowly, the blood, thickening with coagulation, sticking the sides together. Jefferson found it unsettlingly like opening a tissue after blowing your nose. He reached down, grabbed the leg by the ankle and lifted it off the shining surface.

It slipped in his hands and dropped back onto the ground with a dull thud, sending a splash of blood onto Jefferson's bare feet and legs.

This is not real.

He reached down and picked it back up and got it inside the bag.

He didn't follow the trail back to the center this time. He looked up from this post, squinting with his one open eye in the glare of the unbloodied space between this post and the one ahead. The man's right arm, wrist strapped to the rope, was bent at the elbow and resting, a morbid letter V, on some of the unfurled rope.

With one hand holding the knife, the other the sagging bag, Jefferson kept his eyes on the post and started across the shining surface.

As he came level with the group, he heard them talking amongst themselves. They were no longer really paying attention to what he was doing. He wondered what people talk about after committing such a heinous act.

I wonder what's for lunch? Could that *possibly be it?*

Or, maybe, they're discussing what they're going to do to me.

He stopped at the post and cut the rope. He knelt over the arm. He couldn't break his eyes away from the dead man's hand. There was something so undeniably human about a hand. There was blood spattered on it but it was mostly un-covered.

There's the thumb. There's the pointer finger. The middle.

Then Jefferson saw that the man did not have a ring or pinky finger. Just little stubs where they should've been. He felt a phantom twinge in his missing fingers, the same missing fingers on his right hand, and clenched it into a fist. He could almost feel the bite of the nails of those missing fingers in his palm.

Oh. God.

Jefferson knew he had to keep moving. They were wait-ing. Taking up the dead man's limb by the hand was too much. He couldn't do it. He reached down and took up the arm by the forearm. He peeled the bag back open—this time it made a sickeningly wet noise as the sides slowly came apart—and let the arm drop onto the two legs.

He rose to his feet, his knees popping like muted firecrack-ers, and crossed the shining surface to the last post and the arm that waited.

He turned his head slightly, trying to steal an unseen glance at the group.

They were watching again.

He jerked his head forward and picked up his pace.

The arm was extended, the hand palm up as if in supplica-tion. The wrist was longer than it should've been. The pulling of the rope must have dislocated it from the rest of the fore-arm.

Jefferson cut the rope and picked up the arm. He tried not to look at the hand but he did. It was missing the thumb and pointer finger.

Jefferson's stomach dropped. He felt full of squirming worms. They were in every part of him, crawling, trying to get out.

He opened the bag and found it nearly full. He had to

reach into the bloody mess and rearrange the limbs there like some horrific game of Tetris. He had to shove, feared the bag would break, but, finally, got the arm in.

There was no way to tie the bag. He just had to grip it at the tops like an overstuffed, cheap garbage bag.

He turned around, careful not to slip in the thickening blood, and started back to the center of the crater.

His mind was oddly empty. He tried to will it toward some semblance of thought but it too felt full of worms. Things crawling. That's all he could think about. There were things inside him crawling around, possibly feeding on whatever was in their way. His intestines. His lungs. His testicles. His brain.

Worms.

She extended her hand for the bag. Jefferson lifted it in both of his hands and held it out. She took it.

There was a narrow staircase, also coated with the shining material of the rest of the crater, that led up and out. Jefferson didn't think he could've found it had he been left in the center of the crater on his own; it blended in perfectly with the rest of the thing.

They ascended, one by one, She in front of Jefferson, Jefferson bringing up the rear. The last man out. He turned around halfway up and stared down at the blackened spot in the center. The lump, the dim shape of a limbless man. It seemed so far away and so fantastic it could've very well have been a mirage.

Jefferson turned around and followed She out into the mercifully dim forest.

The shade of the overhanging trees brought goosebumps rippling across Jefferson's body. The blood over the entirety of his front half was drying and the stretching of the skin brought a wave of nausea washing over him. It felt like the worms were eating their way out of him. Thousands of tiny, eyeless heads full of miniscule teeth were tearing their way out of his face, his neck, his chest, arms, stomach, legs, feet.

Jefferson stopped walking. He hunched over, his hands raking at every inch of his blood covered skin he could touch. His eye watered over and squeezed shut.

Oh God. The worms.

The vomit erupted from him. He hadn't felt it coming. It caught him by surprise and he wasn't able to ready himself, to clench his muscles and hold his bowels in. He felt piss and shit streak down his thighs, front and back. He felt it run down his legs, mingling with the blood there.

He threw up again and again.

An immense pressure filled his head. He felt like his eyes would literally pop out of his head despite the twine keeping them closed.

He ran out of substance to expel. He retched and farted and belched.

Someone, a man's voice, laughed from the path ahead.

He didn't bother trying to clean himself. When he could manage it, Jefferson simply started back up the path through the forest.

He walked. He felt the worms slowing. Many had already eaten their way out of him. He pictured the inside of his body as that of a rotted jack-o'-lantern the week after Halloween.

They were well ahead of him. He saw She's back, straight and erect and flowing with her fluid, sure-footed strides. Ahead of her he saw the general shape of the group. Chanters. Debts and bad pain. They had just killed a man.

How many have they killed?

He felt empty. He knew he would eventually die. He knew it would not be in his sleep as an old, wealthy man. He knew it would not be in a car crash. He knew it wouldn't be by some hereditary illness.

No. I will die here. By the hands of these people. Debts and bad pain.

The path ahead opened and Jefferson saw the ocean waiting. Sun reflected off the glistening sand-covered beach. One by one the group stepped out into the light. Jefferson watched She as she went. Her feet sunk into the sand but her pace did not slow. She didn't seem to be working extra despite the sand's resistance but Jefferson knew her body was.

Jefferson, covered in shit and piss and blood, stepped into the warm sand and closed his partially sewn-up left eye. The sun, beating down from the cloudless sky, was red and hot behind his closed lids. It felt like he was completely submerged in a warming kettle of blood. For a moment, he was sure he was being cooked alive in the blood of others.

"Go clean yourself," She said.

He didn't move his head in her direction. Jefferson, eyes still closed, walked dumbly to the sound of the gently lapping water ahead. The sand thickened then became more packed then cold and wet under his toes. His feet met the water. He felt a wave break against his thighs, just above his knees. He pushed his legs forward against the resistance of the incoming water.

He kept his eyes closed.

He waded out until the water was up to his chest then he dropped to his knees. The water lifted his arms. He let his body go. He let the water do with him as it pleased.

Acknowledgments

Big thanks to Carrie and Grindhouse Press for taking the chance on this strange, brutal story. I'd also like to thank Andersen Prunty for his excellent editing work.

A.S. Coomer is a writer, musician and perpetual rain dog. His work has appeared in over forty literary journals, magazines, anthologies and the like. He was nominated for the Pushcart Prize three times in 2016. His debut novel, Rush's Deal (Hammer & Anvil Books), came out December 11th, 2016. The Fetishists is his second novel. You can find him at www.ascoomer.com.

Other Grindhouse Press Titles

#666__Satanic Summer by Andersen Prunty

#030__Ritualistic Human Sacrifice by C.V. Hunt

#029__The Atrocity Vendor by Nick Cato

#028__Burn Down the House and Everyone In It by Zachary T. Owen

#027__Misery and Death and Everything Depressing by C.V. Hunt

#026__Naked Friends by Justin Grimbol

#025__Ghost Chant by Gina Ranalli

#024__Hearers of the Constant Hum by William Pauley III

#023__Hell's Waiting Room by C.V. Hunt

#022__Creep House: Horror Stories by Andersen Prunty

#021__Other People's Shit by C.V. Hunt

#020__The Party Lords by Justin Grimbol

#019__Sociopaths In Love by Andersen Prunty

#018__The Last Porno Theater by Nick Cato

#017__Zombieville by C.V. Hunt

#016__Samurai Vs. Robo-Dick by Steve Lowe

#015__The Warm Glow of Happy Homes by Andersen Prunty

#014__How To Kill Yourself by C.V. Hunt

#013__Bury the Children in the Yard: Horror Stories by Andersen Prunty

#012 __Return to Devil Town (Vampires in Devil Town Book Three) by Wayne Hixon

#011__Pray You Die Alone: Horror Stories by Andersen Prunty

#010__King of the Perverts by Steve Lowe

#009__Sunruined: Horror Stories by Andersen Prunty

#008__Bright Black Moon (Vampires in Devil Town Book

Two) by Wayne Hixon

#007__Hi I'm a Social Disease: Horror Stories by Andersen Prunty

#006__A Life On Fire by Chris Bowsman

#005__The Sorrow King by Andersen Prunty

#004__The Brothers Crunk by William Pauley III

#003__The Horribles by Nathaniel Lambert

#002__Vampires in Devil Town by Wayne Hixon

#001__House of Fallen Trees by Gina Ranalli

#000__Morning is Dead by Andersen Prunty

CPSIA information can be obtained
at www.ICGtesting.com
Printed in the USA
LVHW112026190822
726385LV00004B/255